THE FIRE OF LIFE

THE FIRE OF LIFE

Hilary Wilde

CHIVERS

British Library Cataloguing in Publication Data available

This Large Print edition published by AudioGO Ltd, Bath, 2012.
Published by arrangement with the Author.

U.K.   Hardcover   ISBN   978 1 4713 0632 7
U.K.   Softcover   ISBN   978 1 4713 0633 4

Printed and bound in Great Britain by
MPG Books Group Limited

CHAPTER ONE

As Rayanne sank into the chair with a sigh of relief, Mike Crisp, a sun-tanned man with fair hair and a pointed beard, smiled sympathetically. He was Chief Warden of the Jefferson Wild Life Reserve and had driven to the small African airport to meet her.

'Tired?' he asked. 'You've come a long way in a short time. You're here, I understand, to write a thesis on wild life conservation?'

Rayanne nodded wearily. 'Yes . . .' and wondered if she was quite mad to have flown over six thousand miles to do so. Even if she succeeded, which she doubted, what would it really prove?

She felt a mess; hot, sticky, her short, curly, honey-coloured hair was thick with dust, her leaf-green linen coat and dress both crumpled. She found it hard to breathe, the air was so humid, she just longed for a cold drink and to be able to relax in a hot bath.

'I saw Mr Jefferson's Rover outside, so he must be in my office,' Mike Crisp said. 'I'll tell him you're here.'

He went through the door that led into the single-floored house from the wide *stoep* running all round it. The garden outside was ablaze with crimson, yellow and blue flowers. Rayanne closed her eyes wearily.

'I was a fool to agree to have her.' A deep impatient masculine voice jerked her awake. 'These girls are nothing but headaches.'

Her sleepiness vanished and became dismay as she realised she had unwittingly gone into the same atmosphere she had known and hated at home. An atmosphere in which she was just a *dumb blonde*, a stupid moron with no brains, and now she was 'nothing but a headache'. She had hoped that leaving home might land her in an environment where girls were accepted as equals, but it seemed she had failed. She wanted to get up and run away, but how could she? Driving through the Reserve in the Land Rover, she had seen enormous elephants strolling along, swinging their huge trunks, and the lions were looking up as they passed. She was caught . . . for how could she escape?

The door swung open and two men stood there. She stared at them. They stared at her. She had no idea what she had expected to see, but Cary Jefferson was completely different from what his angry, impatient voice had suggested. He was tall, much taller than Mike Crisp, as broad-shouldered, with the same deeply tanned skin, his black hair cut short, his eyes dark.

A smile lit up his grave face. 'I hope you're not too tired, Miss Briscoe,' he said gently as he stared at the quaint, three-cornered face. There was fear—or was it hostility in her

2

eyes? he wondered. 'It can be a tiring journey and I gather the road through the Reserve was pretty bad.' He turned to Mike. 'I'll leave Miss Briscoe in your efficient hands, Mike. The hostels are closed, so she'd better go in one of the rondavels.'

Rayanne saw the quick dismay on Mike Crisp's face. 'But . . .'

'It's the only answer, Mike.' There was a new note in Cary Jefferson's voice, a note of authority, perhaps arrogance? Rayanne thought. 'Please apologise to Samantha for not letting her know earlier.' He turned to the girl waiting, her mouth dry, her eyes smarting. 'You need a good rest, Miss Briscoe. I'll come along tomorrow and show you around.'

This time Mike Crisp turned to him. 'When will Mrs Jefferson be back?' he asked.

'Any moment now,' Cary Jefferson shrugged. 'You know what she's like—here today and gone tomorrow. I expect her when I see her.'

'You'll be glad to have her back,' said Mike. It was a statement, not a question.

'I most certainly will,' Cary Jefferson laughed. 'I try not to worry about her, but she does such stupid things.'

Rayanne stiffened. What a strange man he was! He could be charming, and apparently considerate, and the next moment making fun of his wife. Of course he must be married, for anyone so attractive and handsome as Cary

3

Jefferson would be married before his mid-thirties. He turned to speak to her. 'You need a hot bath, a cool drink and a long sleep, Miss Briscoe, and you'll feel a different person. I'll see you in the morning. Cheers, Mike. I'll phone you later.'

'Yes,' Mike said slowly. The screened door closed with a sharp little bang and Mike smiled ruefully. 'Better sit down, Miss Briscoe. I must go and break it to the wife.'

'Break it?' Rayanne began, but Mike had vanished into the house. Rayanne sat down slowly and sighed. What was the corny old phrase? *Out of the frying pan into the fire?* She had escaped from her home only to land where women were, obviously, a 'headache'. But how could Mr Jefferson speak like that about his wife? It didn't make sense, because he was polite, so . . . she sighed. She knew she should never have come, never have listened to Uncle Joe.

She wondered what Mike Crisp's wife would be like. He had said some funny words: 'Break it'. Break what? The news that she had an unwanted guest? Rayanne moved uncomfortably. She really had got herself in a mess.

Then she heard voices. A female voice.

'It's all very well for him to apologise, but I'm getting sick and tired of this! He must have known she was coming. Yes, I know *we* knew, but I took it for granted she'd either stay with

4

Miss Macintyre or Miss Horlock, if not in the hostel. Why she has to go into one of those ghastly rondavels . . .'

The door opened and Rayanne looked up nervously. Mike Crisp had seemed nice and friendly, but his wife . . .?

Again, Rayanne had a surprise. She certainly had not expected to see such an elegant, beautiful girl as Mike Crisp's wife was, with her long legs in crimson slacks, a white blouse, and her blonde hair piled elaborately on her head, and surprisingly dark eyes.

Rayanne stood up. 'I'm sorry if I'm being a nuisance.'

Surprisingly, Samantha Crisp laughed. 'You are, but I don't blame *you*. It's the boss—he expected us to do the impossible. Anyhow, not to worry, I've told the boy to switch on the geyser. I'll show you to your rondavel. This way.'

Mike Crisp smiled rather ruefully, almost apologetically, at Rayanne, so she smiled back before she followed his wife. Through a long narrow hall that went the length of the building, then out through a stable door, the top half open to the glaring heat of the sun. Through the door, down six steps and along a path that led to a group of round cottages with thatched roofs.

'You're an intellectual, I take it,' Samantha said over her shoulder. 'Come straight from University to study for your thesis? Where's it

5

going to get you?'

'I . . .' Rayanne hesitated and then was honest. 'I don't know.'

Samantha laughed. 'As good an excuse as any! Lucky you had an uncle like Sir Joe Letherington or you'd never have got here. The boss is selective.'

'I gather he sees women as a headache,' said Rayanne.

Samantha laughed again. 'That's what he says!'

'I hear Mrs. Jefferson is away.'

'Yes, she's an old darling. Fusses like mad, but it slides off the boss's back like water off a duckling.'

'An old darling,' Rayanne was thinking, shocked and surprised, for Cary Jefferson wasn't the type of man to marry an older woman, surely?

Samantha went on, still talking over her shoulder as the path was too narrow for two to walk abreast.

'Of course she's going on for eighty, now, though you wouldn't think it the way she prances around.'

Rayanne began to laugh. 'I didn't know we were talking about his mother. I thought it was his wife.'

'His wife?' Samantha snorted. 'He'll never marry. He's too clever. Not that we're ever short of girls chasing him and finding excuses to come here.' She turned her head and

6

narrowed her eyes as she looked at Rayanne. 'Is that why you're here? If so, you're wasting your time. You haven't a hope.'

Rayanne's face burned. 'Of course it isn't! I had no idea . . . I mean I thought Mr Jefferson was an older man, the way Uncle Joe talked. Incidentally, he's my godfather, no real relation.'

Samantha chuckled. 'I've heard that story before. No idea! This first one is yours. All the other rondavels are empty at the moment.'

The unusual-looking round little one-room cottage was clean. It had a thatched roof, stable door, and was freshly painted. Samantha opened the door and led the way inside. It was cool and quite light with two windows, mosquito-netted, a single bed, a table and a chair and a fold-up garden chair.

'There's a communal bathroom just along here,' Samantha explained, leading the way.

'It's a . . . a bit lonely,' Rayanne said diffidently, not wanting to admit fear.

Her companion chuckled. 'Not to worry, we have a very good night-watchman with a ferocious dog. Scares the liver out of anyone who comes near. Now watch out for snakes. Don't for heaven's sake walk into that long grass.'

They were standing outside the communal bathroom now. The glare made Rayanne's eyes smart. The long grass seemed to surround them, coming close to the narrow path. The land sloped gradually down in front of them and she could just see the turgid brown water through the trees that lined the river.

'Snakes,' Samantha went on cheerfully. 'Not that they attack you—only the dangerous kind. Just never walk through long grass, because if you frighten them or step on them, they'll bite you. If they do, race like mad for the house and we'll give you an injection quickly. Has to be fast or it could be fatal.'

'I won't go in the grass,' Rayanne said quickly, trying not to shiver. 'No wild animals about?'

Samantha laughed. 'No. We're safely fenced off. Oh, except for the crocodiles.' She waved her hand dramatically towards the river. 'We have crocodiles at the bottom of our garden,' she chanted.

'Not really?'

'Yes, really. You're in no danger, though, unless you go for a swim, and if you did a stupid thing like that, you deserve to be caught.'

'Do . . . do people get caught?'

'If they're fools. The piccanins play in the water sometimes or their mothers wash their clothes and don't watch out. Well, I'll leave you to unpack. I see Moses has brought down your luggage. The bath should be hot in twenty minutes. Then have a sleep. Better come up to the house about five and we'll have a drink before we eat. Mike will bring you home, because it can be pretty scaring in the dark.'

'And that's no lie,' Rayanne thought miserably as Samantha hurried back towards the house. 'It's pretty scaring in daylight!'

Once inside her rondavel, she unpacked, keeping an eye on her watch. She longed to lie in the hot water, to wash her dusty hair, her aching limbs. When twenty minutes was up, she seized her dressing-gown and put it on and made her way to the small immaculately-clean bathroom. She locked the door and turned on the tap, then froze with horror. She could not believe her eyes.

The water was brown. *Muddy river water.* How could she ever wash her face in that?

*   *   *

Later, after Rayanne had bathed reluctantly, then drank gratefully the iced lemonade Samantha had sent down to the rondavel, and had slept for several hours, Samantha, greeting Rayanne in the doorway, confessed that she had forgotten to warn her about the muddy water.

'Sorry about that,' Samantha said briskly. She had changed into a many-coloured kaftan; now her hair hung down her back in soft curls. 'I should have warned you. Fair makes you sick, doesn't it? By the way, don't ever drink it, will you? That way you could only get bilharzia. A nasty illness, that—can kill you. I'll

9

send down a jug of drinking water in case you get thirsty in the night.'

She led the way indoors. It was quite an attractive house, Rayanne thought, but she wondered if she would like to live in it—perched above the muddy river, gazing out on to trees of every kind and long grass, with a small garden fighting for existence and in the distance, the mountains, changing colour as the sun began to go down slowly. The lounge was newly decorated, the walls a pale lilac shade: the chairs and couch had yellow silk covers. Samantha poured them each a sherry and they sat down.

'Nice to have someone who's not a ghastly intellectual to talk to,' she began, then her face screwed up. 'I forgot—*you're* an intellectual, too. Straight from university with all the long words, I don't doubt.'

Rayanne laughed. 'Some of them do really go to extremes, don't they? I can't bear that kind of talk.'

'Nor me, neither,' Samantha laughed. 'How do you like to live here?

Rayanne hesitated, looking round. 'It's a very nice house ...'

'Exactly,' Samantha said triumphantly. 'That's all that can be said. It's a nice house, it's a nice house! "You're lucky, you are, my girl," that's what they say. No, "my *dear* girl," of course. "Lots of women would be grateful," but I'm not lots of women. I want to live, not

10

vegetate. I'd never have married Mike if I'd known life was to be like this. Tricked me, he did, all right. I thought he was interested in trees—forests, you know. I guessed we'd be off to Canada or British Columbia or somewhere exciting like that, but oh no, oh dear me, no,' she said bitterly. Mike meets up with the boss and before you can say "Bob's your uncle" we were on our way out here.'

Mike came in, yawning. 'Oh, dry up, darling,' he said. 'You're boring Miss Briscoe to tears. You know it's not as bad as you make out. I'm earning good money, we're not spending it.'

'You're telling me, Mike! Never a gay moment do I have. No one to talk to . . .'

Mike straightened, his glass in hand. 'Look, Samantha, you know very well you can go to any of the socials. You refuse, but . . .'

'And why? You know why. All those girls with their hoity-toity words and that condescending grin. They talk all the time. I never get a chance to say a word.' She swung round to look at Rayanne. 'It'll be interesting to see how you get on with them, Miss Briscoe. You'll have to be tough or they'll just swamp you.'

'Samantha, please! Miss Briscoe isn't a student. She need have nothing to do with them.'

'Well, if she's got any sense, she'll keep away from them or they'll finish her off all

11

right,' Samantha said angrily. 'I must go and see how the dinner's going. Dorcas has no idea at all . . .'

Alone, Mike and Rayanne smiled at one another. 'Poor Samantha,' Mike said. 'She really does hate it here. Trouble is, I love it. This is my work and, as I said, I get good money and am saving for our future. Samantha would like me to drop everything and walk out and find another job. I can't help feeling that wherever we go, she'll be fed up with it.'

'I should think it could be very lonely,' Rayanne said carefully.

Mike jumped up, took her empty glass to refill it. 'I don't find it so,' he said cheerfully. 'But then I'm the type that can adjust. Unfortunately Samantha can't.'

'Talking about me?' Samantha asked, coming in quickly, looking alert.

'I was just saying, darling, that you and I are different types,' Mike said soothingly. 'That's why we get on so well. We complement one another.'

'Compliment? You never pay me compliments,' Samantha said bitterly, and Rayanne saw that Samantha had got hold of the wrong word.

'I expect if you always look as you are tonight, he just expects it of you. How do you manage to be so glamorous?' Rayanne asked.

Samantha's face relaxed. 'You like my hair down?' She turned in a circle, her hair

12

swinging. 'I've got to keep myself up to my standards or else I'll just . . . well, go to bits. Yes, Mike, another drink, please.'

Slowly the evening dragged by, or so it did to Rayanne, though Samantha seemed to enjoy it, talking away, constantly speaking angrily about 'the boss'. At last Rayanne, pleading a headache, was taken down through the dark night by Mike, who had two torches.

'I'll leave you with one, because at midnight your electricity is switched off automatically. If you hear someone outside, don't worry. It's the watchman. He may look rather alarming, but I assure you he's to be trusted. He has a dog with him who sometimes growls or barks.'

'Do crocodiles walk ashore?' Rayanne asked as he led the way, the torch throwing a beam of light on the narrow path ahead. It was a hot humid night with small insects buzzing round her face.

'Only up on to the sandbanks. Samantha told you about them?' Mike sounded annoyed. 'She delights in scaring people. I can assure you that no crocodile could get up to this height.'

'Or . . . or snakes?'

'Very unlikely. Maybe you noticed that there was a wide band of small stones round the rondavel. This keeps away snakes. It's where people allow creepers or shrubs to grow up close to the windows that snakes get in. You scared?'

Rayanne managed a laugh. *The understatement of the year?* It was another corny phrase, yet it described the words exactly. 'In a way. It's all so strange.'

'You'll adjust. It's amazing what you can get used to when you have no choice,' Mike said cheerfully, unlocking her rondavel, opening the door, switching on the light.

After he had left her, first checking that a tray with iced water, a thermos of boiling water, a cup and saucer, coffee, sugar and milk was on the table by her bedside, Rayanne thought of his words.

'It's amazing what you can get used to when you have no choice.' How right he was: *when you have no choice!* Had Cary Jefferson deliberately put her in this horrible rondavel in order to scare her? she wondered. Was this his sly method of getting rid of her? He had said she was a ' headache'. Perhaps this was part of his plan.

Well, if so, his plan was going to fail, she told herself as she undressed, carefully putting the torch under her pillow, for after midnight there would be no light.

Once in bed, she switched off the light and lay hugging the torch as if it was the proverbial teddy-bear. How quiet it was! She could hear the mosquitoes banging against the screens on the window. Perhaps they could scent her, for there was no light to attract them. Some frogs began croaking. Then quiet again. Then

14

suddenly a loud buzzing, rather like a hive of bees let loose. The cicadas, of course! She was nearly asleep when a nerve-shattering howl broke the quietness. In a moment, the howling came again. It was closer. Another howl and again it was even still closer. Her hand shaking, Rayanne fumbled for the bedside lamp switch. Nothing happened. Only the darkness stayed. She switched on the torch . . .

Again nothing happened. The batteries must have run out, for there was only darkness still.

CHAPTER TWO

In the morning, Rayanne looked at her reflection anxiously. It had been a terribly frightening night in which she had hardly slept, hugging the useless torch, listening to the strange night cries. She was sure she had heard a lion roaring—and an elephant trumpeting anger. A flash of light had shone through her windows several times, frightening her until she heard a dog bark and knew it was the night watchman. Not that he was much comfort, for he was only walking by and soon gone. Never in all her life had she been so frightened.

And it showed in her pale face, her red tired eyes with the dark shadows below them. Somehow she must hide that. Cary Jefferson must not be allowed to win, or even know how near winning he had been! In the night, she had sworn she would leave in the morning. But now the sun was bright and warm, making the brown river sparkle as she looked out of the window and saw the huge red flowers on the flamboyants, and could smell the delicious scent from the white gardenias behind the rondavel, and she knew that somehow or other, she must stick it out. She could just imagine her brothers' teasing if she went home the day after she arrived at the Reserve.

'We knew you'd never make it,' they'd say triumphantly.

And her father would shake his head sadly. 'I told you this was no life for a girl. It's work for a man with his strength and brains.'

And perhaps her mother would say very quietly: 'I don't blame you, Rayanne, I'd have been scared stiff, too.'

No, she had to stay, Rayanne knew that. Maybe Mike was right and in a little while she would adjust. She had to. She had no choice.

Half an hour later, she made her way to the house where breakfast was waiting. Samantha smiled, her eyes amused.

'Well, what sort of a night did you have? Manage to sleep?'

Rayanne forced a bright smile. 'It took a while to get to sleep, but then I slept like a log.'

16

'Heard the hyenas howling? They were really bad last night,' Mike said, helping himself to toast.

Rayanne mentally made a note of that hopeful, helpful news. So the hyenas didn't howl every night. One blessing.

It was at ten o'clock that Cary Jefferson called for her. He was wearing what she had learned was known as a safari suit. He looked incredibly handsome, even more so when he smiled, yet she was on her guard. He had deliberately put her in the hateful rondavel to try to frighten her. No doubt he was waiting to enjoy his victory. Well, he could wait, she told herself, as she smiled sweetly at him and said she had slept well.

'A most comfortable rondavel and Samantha looked after me,' Rayanne said brightly.

Cary smiled. 'I'm glad. Samantha is a wonderful hostess.'

He led the way to the Land Rover and helped her in. Before he started the engine, he turned to her.

'You'll be given a Rover and can go wherever you like for the research you plan to do—but there's one thing, Miss Briscoe, and on this I must insist.' He looked down at her gravely. 'You are not to go out in the Land Rover alone. Is that clearly understood? I'll let you have one of the Rangers and he must always go with you.'

'But why?' she asked quickly, sensing patronage in his words. 'I mean, I'd never get out of the Rover, of course. Does everyone have to take a Ranger with him?'

A slight movement of Cary's mouth made her think he was amused. 'No, not everyone,' he said gently. 'Only girls.'

'But why girls? I don't need protection. I promise you I'd do nothing stupid.'

He turned his body round on the seat so that he could look down on her more comfortably.

'Look, Miss Briscoe, suppose the Rover broke down. Would you enjoy getting out in the midst of a crowd of lions to cope with the problem? That's why you're to take a trained mechanic who is also a Ranger with you. Is that understood?'

Rayanne frowned as she looked at him. Yet he was right.

'I understand,' she said reluctantly.

It seemed to be his turn to frown as he looked at her. She was wearing white jeans and a vividly striped black and white blouse.

'Very attractive outfit,' he said thoughtfully, 'but hardly suitable for this. I suggest you run along to your rondavel and change into something else—brown, black, navy blue, or khaki.'

Instantly she was on the defensive. 'What's wrong with what I'm wearing?'

He smiled. 'Nothing, but it's not for *now*. I

quite sympathise with you, Miss Briscoe. A small person has to wear something strikingly startling or else she—or he—will never be noticed, but I would prefer a little less publicity this time. The monkeys are attracted by bright colours and can be a darned nuisance. Do you mind?'

She hesitated. He had no right to criticise . . . yet he had, in a way. After all, he knew more about the Reserve than she did.

'I'll be as quick as I can,' she promised.

She almost tripped up as she ran fast to her rondavel, hastily changing into a pair of dull dark blue jeans and a matching blouse. She looked in the mirror and saw that some of her whiteness had gone. Anger, obviously, was doing her good.

As she hurried back to the Land Rover she wondered if she had a right to be angry. After all, Cary Jefferson was right about the danger of a Land Rover breaking down. She shivered at the thought of it happening and a great crowd of enormous elephants coming along the road towards her! This would be a time in which she would need a man, not only able to make the engine go, or change the tyre but to protect her as well. As for the clothes—! She hadn't been sure what sort of appointment she would have with Mr Jefferson and, thinking he might be going to introduce her to the rest of the staff, some of whom sounded ghastly, according to Samantha, she had thought she should dress up.

As she reached the Land Rover, Cary smiled, 'You were quick!'

'Well trained,' she said. 'Five brothers.'

'Help!' he laughed as he started the engine. 'No sisters?'

'None. Dad wanted six sons. I was a disappointment.' Without realising it, her voice was wistful. It had always hurt her, the knowledge that she had disappointed her parents. They made no secret of it. She had disappointed them in so many ways, for she had only just scraped through her exams while her brothers had got Honours. All five were lawyers. Only she was drifting, not knowing what she wanted to do. It had been Uncle Joe's suggestion that she write a thesis on wild life conservation that had seemed the answer.

Glancing quickly at the man by her side, she was no longer sure that it was. The Land Rover bumped over the earth road and went through the gate of the wire fence to the main road.

'I'll introduce you to the staff first,' Cary Jefferson said cheerfully, and Rayanne knew dismay. It was just as she had thought! He had made her change into these drab clothes and look a fright and then let her meet the staff members that Mrs Crisp disliked so much! What would they think of her? Had he done it on purpose? To cut her down to size? she wondered.

Again she quickly glanced at him. His profile was almost more handsome than his full face, with that square chin, the rather large nose and the arrogant lift to his head. He was whistling softly. She seemed to know the tune, but could not name it.

Was he resenting her? she wondered. Was she wasting his precious time? Yet why had he to show her round? Surely Mike Crisp could have done it? Or was Uncle Joe's influence on Cary Jefferson so strong?

Later she was to realise that she had been so wrapped up in self-pity and resentment that she hardly noticed the beauty of the house they reached, a long L-shaped white house with the usual wide *stoep*. She could see the river below, much closer than at the rondavel where she had slept, or rather tried to sleep! There was a sloping lawn down to the water, shaded by tall red-flowered flamboyant trees, and she could see sandbanks on the side of the still dark brown water. Something on one of them moved!

'Are there crocodiles there?' she asked as Cary Jefferson stopped the car before the house.

He turned and looked at her, his eyes amused. 'Of course there are. Scared?'

'Of course not,' she said indignantly.

'Well, I am. Scared of people taking foolish risks.' He opened the door of the Land Rover.

'I've got to fetch some keys. Won't be a

moment,' he said, and left her.

She looked round curiously. This was obviously his home, where he lived, apparently, with his mother. Now she could see it was a beautifully-designed house with large windows shaded against the hot glare of the sun by venetian blinds. Several Africans were working in the garden, and glanced at her without interest.

Cary Jefferson joined her and started the engine, driving round the tall weeping willow that grew in the centre of the circular parking space.

'Know what the croc does to his victim?' Cary said cheerfully as they left the garden and were back on the main road, trees and bushes growing closely on either side. He did not wait for her answer. 'They drag him under water to a shelf at the side of the river they've prepared, then leave the body there until it rots before they eat it.'

Before she could control it, a shiver passed through Rayanne.

'Oh no!' she said.

Cary Jefferson chuckled. 'Oh yes. I'm surprised you didn't know that!' His voice changed suddenly. 'Just what interest have you in nature conservation?' he asked sternly.

Rayanne was startled. 'Well, I . . . I was always interested in wild life, biology, conservation . . . and when Uncle Joe told me of the wonderful job you were doing out here, he suggested . . .'

'It was his suggestion, not yours?' Cary Jefferson asked curtly.

'Oh yes. You see . . . you see I didn't know what I . . . well . . .' Rayanne stumbled over the words, trying not to sound too stupid, wishing she had never left the shores of England.

Again he startled her, for he smiled. 'I see. You were just at that stage we all go through when we've gone so far and can't be sure where to go on. I went through it. Can you imagine it? I was a stockbroker originally.'

'You weren't?' Rayanne turned to stare at him, at his dark sun-tanned skin, his safari suit with open collar and short sleeves. 'I can't see you in an office!'

He laughed. 'You're so right. That's how I felt. Then as a kid, I'd always been interested in the fast diminishing wild life of this country and used to spend all my money going to the game reserves. At one time, I wanted to be a game warden, but my father was ill and I didn't want to leave home. Then he died, so I told my mother I wanted to start my own wild life reserve and finally persuaded her I had to do it or be a crazy, mixed-up kid for the whole of my life. So we came up here, built the house, and slowly everything else.'

Ahead of them was a tall narrow building. 'That's Jefferson Hall,' Cary Jefferson told her. 'That's where we lecture.'

He drove past it and she saw three square

23

two-storied houses in a row, joined by glassed-in corridors. He stopped the Land Rover and she slid out so that she was ready when he came to her side.

'This middle house is where they eat, have games and study. On the left is the hostel for boys, on the far right the hostel for girls. Actually we get a surprising number of girls interested in conservation. I've often wondered why.'

'And why shouldn't they be interested?' Rayanne asked quickly.

She saw the smile playing round his mouth as he stared down at her. 'And why should they?'

'Oh!' She tried to control her quick anger, but the Irish blood in her was coming out. 'Why must you men always differentiate between men and women? Why shouldn't a woman be interested in wild life?'

'Two simple reasons, my dear child.'

Rayanne's hand ached as she kept it from smacking his smug face.

'Name them,' she challenged.

'Well, first men and women are physically different. Man is much stronger . . .'

'That's absolute tripe! We're as strong as you. How many men could have six children and run a house without breaking down? I wonder how many men would have the second child. Once would be enough!'

He was obviously trying not to laugh. 'It
24

might be the answer to the problem of the world's fast-growing population. My second reason is that it's a lonely life, hard work, and not very well rewarded financially.'

'You think women work only for money?' Rayanne was having a hard fight with her temper, but she tried to steady her voice.

Cary threw back his head and laughed. 'My, my, Ray, you do bite the bait! I was only teasing you. In any case, let's be honest, don't you think women require financial security more than men?'

She wasn't sure whether to be angry with him or share in his laughter. Why hadn't she recognised the signs? He had only been teasing her—just as her brothers did. And just as she did with them, she had risen to the bait!

'I don't know. I've never been very poor,' she said thoughtfully. 'I think if I had children, I would want financial security.'

'You want children?'

Startled, Ryanne looked at him. 'Of course I do. I'd like four, but I'll be content with two. One of each.'

'Are you engaged—or in love?'

She stiffened, because it was none of his business. She glared at him. 'No, I'm not engaged . . .' she began angrily, and then hesitated. Staring at him, his face seemed to blur for a moment and then came back, each item on his face brilliantly outlined. Her hand ached again, but this time to touch his face

25

gently, to trace those thick dark eyebrows, the prominent nose, the square chin, his ears with their slightly big lobes but that lay flat against his head. 'No,' she said unsteadily, 'I'm not in love .. at least ....'

'Good, so you won't be getting long phone calls from your beloved,' Cary said, taking her arm. 'We'll go to the Clinic first.'

Stumbling a little, for though it was absurd, Rayanne knew, her legs felt weak and she longed for a cup of tea or even something stronger. Perhaps it was the altitude, the different climate. It was so humid, so still the air!

The Clinic consisted of a small room with a couch, a waiting room that was much bigger, and the Sister's office and locked cupboard of drugs, etc.

A tall slim girl with dark hair came to meet them. 'Cary, how nice to see you,' she said eagerly. 'I've got a quiet morning for a change.' Then she stopped, staring at Rayanne, her eyes narrowing. 'This is . . . .?'

'Yes, I want to introduce Rayanne Briscoe. I told you Mother's close friend, Sir Joe Letherington, wrote and asked if Miss Briscoe might come here to study our work for her thesis,' Cary Jefferson's voice was friendly yet impersonal. 'Mind if I show her round?'

'Of course not. Glad to meet you, Miss Briscoe,' Sister Daphne Macintyre said in her husky attractive voice, but Rayanne knew that the Sister was not in the least bit glad to see her! She could see Sister Macintyre's eyes noting the drab jeans and dark shirt, and for a moment Rayanne knew hatred of Cary Jefferson. The Sister was beautiful, elegantly dressed in a pale pink nylon overall, and Rayanne felt horribly plain.

She followed Cary Jefferson round the Clinic, listening to his description of the sort of casualties they had.

'More often it's the boys who come to study. They're so keen to prove their strength, they'll do the craziest things and turn up with broken legs or arms.'

'Do you get many injuries from . . . from the animals?' Rayanne asked.

Cary Jefferson looked amused. 'Very few, and those we do are the patients' own fault. Occasionally we get a snake bite, of course.'

Next he took her to what he called 'the Lab'.

'I think you'll like Christine Horlock,' he said as he led the way. 'She's beautiful, but plenty of brains. She isn't suffering from the inferiority complex that Sister Daphne is.'

Startled, Rayanne almost gasped. 'Why should she have an inferiority complex? She's beautiful, and . . .'

'And uneducated. Oh, I'm not saying she isn't educated, but she's the only one of the staff who didn't go to a university, and this smarts. She hates us all.'

'That's absurd! I thought she was very nice,'

27

Rayanne said quickly, as usual leaping to the defence of anyone attacked.

Cary Jefferson chuckled. 'You're a bad liar, Ray,' he said, and pushed open two swinging doors. 'Here we are. Christine!' he called. 'We've come to see you!'

It was a very modern, efficient-looking laboratory, Rayanne saw instantly, and the girl who came to meet them was the same—tall and blonde, with blue eyes and a friendly smile as she held out her hand.

'Welcome, Miss . . . Miss Briscoe. Is that right?' she said, and turned to Cary. 'Not often we see you at this hour, Cary.'

'I'm just showing Ray Briscoe round,' he told her with a smile.

Rayanne stood silently. They seemed to have forgotten her as they stared at one another, both smiling. It was almost as if they were talking, as if through their eyes a message could pass.

Then Cary Jefferson turned to Rayanne. Well, we mustn't waste any of our precious time or that of Christine's . . . I won't be a moment, Ray.'

It was odd—and yet strangely nice—that he called her *Ray*. It was a name no one had ever called her before, Rayanne was thinking as she waited while Cary Jefferson and Christine Horlock looked through a microscope and earnestly discussed something.

What a mixture of different people he was,

Rayanne thought. A real Jekyll and Hyde, only instead of being two people he was about a dozen. She was never sure which one he was going to be; one moment, so relaxed and friendly, then accusing, then understanding, and the next almost condemning her. She felt horribly drab and plain in her clothes. Miss Horlock was wearing a sleeveless white overall and still managed to make it look as if it came from Paris.

Back in the Land Rover again, Cary explained something of the problems.

'Nature conservation isn't only a case of keeping wild animals alive, but it is an applied science,' he began, sounding rather pompous, Rayanne thought as she sat meekly, hands folded, as the Land Rover bounced about the bad earth roads. 'We're continually engaged in observation and research. We leave the academic type to research institutes. Soil conservation means the soil must be protected against exposure as well as erosion and must be chemically treated or it may become impoverished. Dead trees and other vegetation should be allowed to rot rather than be burnt. Water, of course, is another problem. The depth and stability . . .' he went on gravely.

Rayanne listened. At least, she tried to, but she found her thoughts going constantly back to the way Christine Horlock and Cary Jefferson had looked at one another. Were they in love? Perhaps they were without

29

knowing it? Christine Horlock was very beautiful, she also had brains and obviously a deep interest in conservation, so she would make Cary Jefferson a good wife.

They paused as they came to a big double gate that divided the eight-foot-tall wire fence and the African came running to open it, lift his hand in greeting and give a big white-toothed smile as Cary Jefferson spoke to him.

'Why don't you like women visitors?' Rayanne asked as they drove through. She was as startled as he, because she had not meant to ask the question. She felt her cheeks go red. 'I . . . I couldn't help hearing you in the next room.'

Cary laughed. 'Sorry if I sounded inhospitable, but it's happened so often in the past.'

'What's happened?'

He chuckled. 'Well, females can be a headache, because they complain about the heat, the dust, the water. They also talk of their own home with nostalgic reverence, saying what a beautiful place it is, what a fine social life they lead, how very different from this life: this boring, lonely life.'

'It must be boring and lonely for the wife.' Once again, Rayanne leapt to the defence of Samantha Crisp.

'I agree—that's why wardens should be careful before they marry—or cease to be wardens. The trouble is, it's a kind of bug.

30

Getting involved, I mean. You may have heard of a poet called Landor. I don't know if he's well-known, but I always remember a poem I learned at school . . . "I strove with none, for none was worth my strife. Nature I loved, and next to Nature, Art; I warmed both hands before the fire of life. It sinks and I am ready to depart".' He laughed. 'You must think I'm mad, but that's how I feel about Nature. It's so amazingly wonderful, so fascinating to study. Do you know . . .'

As the Land Rover jolted and jerked, going through the well-shrubbed hillocks and sudden little valleys, giving Rayanne glimpses of distant zebras or wildebeest, he talked to her about his work, what he had learned, what he hoped to learn. She listened entranced, for she had never thought of nature conservation in this light before. Finally he paused and sounded apologetic.

'Sorry, I must have bored you to death.'

Rayanne looked at him gravely. 'On the contrary, you've given me an entirely new slant on conservation. I'm afraid I had no idea . . .'

He glanced down at her. 'Good. It means so little to a lot of people. What's the sense in keeping these animals alive, they say.'

'Mike Crisp feels as you do.'

'I know. I wish Samantha could settle down. That's another reason why I don't welcome female visitors, Ray,' Cary went on, using his abbreviation of her Christian name as if it was the most natural thing in the world, as it would be with some men, yet it had not seemed to her that Cary Jefferson was the type of man to call a girl by her Christian name without first asking permission. He had that rather old-fashioned but very nice courtesy you so seldom saw. But she was glad. Every time he called her Ray, a kind of warmth swept through her body, almost as if he was caressing her.

'If she had a baby . . .' Rayanne said slowly.

'That would be the answer, of course. I gather they want one, but . . .' Cary said slowly.

'Do you want children?' Rayanne asked abruptly. After all, he had asked her!

He looked startled.'Honestly I don't know. Never thought about it. In fact, I doubt if I shall ever marry. I want to be free.'

'Free? But lonely?' Rayanne felt suddenly bleak as if the sun had gone behind a cloud.

'Well, yes, maybe as you grow older you need someone around, but I think when you're young and have work you love, that's all you need. I'm talking about men, of course. Women are different.'

Rayanne looked up. There was a wild canary balanced on a slightly swaying branch, its golden breast so bright, the brown body flecked with gold as he sang sweetly.

'What makes you say that? Why do you always say we're different?'

'Because you are.' Cary was driving slowly past a herd of rhinos, but Rayanne was too

32

engrossed in the conversation to pay wild animals much attention. She was amazed at the ease with which she could talk to Cary Jefferson, and the way he was talking to her. Somehow she had not expected it.

'In what way?'

His powerful hands gripped the steering wheel as he deftly negotiated the Rover from the deep ruts.

'In every way. The average woman needs love. A man doesn't. He can sublimate his need by being engrossed in his work. A woman never could. She has this mother streak in her, this protective desire to have someone need her, someone she can be kind to, can . . . well, can make dependent on her. A woman's strength lies in the dependence on her of the man she loves.'

Rayanne turned sideways, tucking her feet under her. 'I don't understand. You mean a woman has to boss a man before she can feel secure?'

He smiled. 'Definitely. Take my mother. She delights in ordering me around, she knows I'm dependent on her.'

'You are?' Rayanne was startled. She would never have thought this great hulk of a man by her side could be a mother's boy.

He roared with laughter. 'She thinks I am, bless her. Seriously, though, isn't it true? A woman likes to believe a man needs her, then she's happy.'

33

'I don't like the way you put it,' Rayanne said slowly. 'You make women sound awful.'

The Land Rover bumped suddenly and she slid down the seat against Cary.

'I'm sorry,' she gasped.

'I'm the one to say that. Afraid the road is bad. Elephants don't help. Look!'

Rayanne obeyed. Straight ahead, crossing their road, if such it could be called, a herd of elephants walked, swinging their long trunks, placing each foot with deliberate rhythm, ignoring the Land Rover that had slowed up.

'Do they ever attack?' she asked.

'Never. Except when one of them is injured and in pain. Then you reverse like mad and don't stop to argue!'

The last one of the elephants crossed the road, swinging his trunk, flapping his ears, turning his head slowly to stare at them and then, as if totally disinterested, following the herd.

Cary started the engine. 'Where were we? Oh yes. Talking about women and men. Obviously I see the way women love men in a different way from you. How would you define a woman's love?'

Her cheeks felt hot. 'I . . . well, I don't really know.' Didn't she? she found herself wondering. She went on, speaking her thoughts aloud. 'I'd want to make the man I love happy. I'd study his work so that we could talk about it, that I could share his problems

34

and understand things better. I'd only want him to be happy. That to me is love.'

There was a strange silence, only broken by the sudden shrill sound of the cicadas.

'I think that's rather wonderful . . .' Cary said softly, and his hands gripped the steering wheel.

'Have you ever been in love? You said no, but I think you have.'

She tensed, afraid he might guess the truth. 'I think . . . I think I have,' she confessed.

He turned to look at her. 'I hope the man will be worthy of your love,' he said gently. 'Ah, there's young Hardwick.'

A Land Rover came bouncing to meet them with a young shirtless man in it whom Cary introduced and who grinned cheerfully at Rayanne.

'Nice to see a girl's face. I'm getting awfully tired of hippos and lions,' he joked, winking at his boss.

Their quiet talking time was over. Cary Jefferson ceased to be the relaxed man and became instead the authoritative, rather pompous boss.

*   *   *

It was a fascinating day, Rayanne thought, as it came near its close. She had met several of the wardens and in some cases where they were married, their wives. One or two seemed

35

happy enough, but several were like Samantha.

'See what I mean?' Cary Jefferson said once as they drove away from a nice little well-furnished house. 'They kept asking you questions about your wonderful life in England. Is it so wonderful?'

She had hesitated. 'I wouldn't like to generalise. I may be unlucky, but mine wasn't wonderful.'

He looked sympathetic. 'Why ever not?'

'Five brothers, all older and brighter than yourself, didn't make life easy. Dad is disappointed in me and Mother . . . well, she just doesn't do anything at all. She just accepts the situation.'

'You can hardly blame that on to England, then.' Cary had sounded amused.

'Quite definitely not. Life . . . don't you think this is a purely personal thing? I mean, some people can be happy anywhere—'

'And others unhappy anywhere. I agree. Would you say you are a happy person?' His eyes had been twinkling as he looked down at her.

'Not, not so far.'

'Tell me, why have you got this chip on your shoulder? I mean, surely your five brothers can't be the monsters you make them out to be. I'd have thought they'd have spoilt their kid sister.'

'Not my brothers,' she said bitterly.

'Know something, Ray?' He had been

36

driving past some emus as he talked and one had decided to chase them, so now Cary was driving fast, glancing over his shoulder and laughing as he spoke, watching the emu with her funny bouncing run follow them. 'I think it's all your fault.'

'My fault?' Rayanne had felt the anger rising in her. Just another example of man's bias. Everything was the woman's fault—never, oh, but never, the man's!

The emu got tired and gave up the chase, so Cary drove more slowly, pointing out the monkeys on the trees, swinging from branch to branch, and the impala racing across the flat background as they heard the sound of the Land Rover's engine.

'Yes, yours,' he went on. 'You've so convinced yourself that you're no good that you're almost scared to open your mouth. Look, Ray, your problem is really simple. You're sensitive and you rise to bait. You're a sitting duck, if I may be corny. You ask to be teased and you rise at once. Anyone told you how much prettier you are when you lose your temper? Maybe that's why we all tease you!'

She had felt her cheeks burning and anger growing. 'I . . . I . . .' she had begun, and then he slowed up.

They were close to a small damn and seven giraffes stood by it, calmly surveying the brown welcoming water. They turned their heads gracefully and looked at the Land Rover.

'Their faces are like poker faces, aren't they?' Cary was saying. He had slid along the seat close to her. She could feel his breath on her cheek. She wanted to yet dared not turn her face, for his mouth would be near hers and . . .

She shivered. It couldn't be true. You didn't fall in love like this. It must be the change of climate, the altitude—there must be a reason, she thought unhappily. Stiffening, she stared at the giraffes and Cary went on talking softly in her ear.

'Amazing how bored and blasé they look, as if the arrogant creatures can find nothing of amusement or interest. Look, ever seen a giraffe drink water? It's a wonderful exhibition of adapting oneself despite handicaps. Just see the way he widens his legs and finally can get his mouth into the water.'

They watched in silence as the giraffe slowly and with great dignity moved his legs apart. He drank without haste while the other giraffes looked at him thoughtfully. A group of zebras had come to join them and were drinking fast.

'The zebras feel safe,' Cary whispered, his breath even more warm on Rayanne's cheek. 'You'll usually find them drinking water near the tall quick-running giraffes. Can you see those guinea-fowl over there? Look up at that baobab tree just above the dam. See it? Well, that tree could be called a game reserve in itself.

'Up in the crown of its foliage you'll find everything—birds, snakes, monkeys, baboons and bats. Most important of all, the guinea-fowl. They're like deer. They know when danger is near and their metallic cackling warns everyone. Isn't nature interesting with its protective measures?'

'Very,' Rayanne had whispered. Oh, was this love? This ache to be in someone's arms? This longing to touch his cheek, to look in his eyes? Yet it was so absurd. Why, she didn't really know him.

Later they had driven past a pair of proud ostriches. Mother and father walked along with stately pride while, racing ahead of them, like small children, were twelve baby ostriches.

'We're pleased with that lot,' Cary said as they watched the adult ostriches look at the Land Rover anxiously and obviously accept it as not dangerous. 'Ostriches are excellent parents. That reminds me, Ray. I know you haven't had time yet to work out what you'll write for your thesis, but might I suggest you consider concentrating on a certain phase of animal life? Gestation and parenthood, for instance. Of course you know that a kangaroo's baby is only an inch long? Hard to believe, isn't it? Maybe you should have gone to Australia—not only could you have studied kangaroos, but found yourself a rich husband.'

The anger had stirred inside her, but she controlled it. He was teasing. So she smiled

39

sweetly at him. 'Maybe I should have,' she said, and saw by the twinkle in his eyes that he had watched with amusement her battle with her temper. One win to her, she had thought. 'Actually, thanks for the suggestion. If I remember rightly, elephants don't reach puberty for ten years and gestation is twenty-two months. It's an awful long time for the poor cow to be pregnant.'

'They seem to accept it. The calf is dependent on the cow for two years, and when he's weaned, he goes off with the bull. Rather interesting, that. Pity mankind doesn't follow the elephant's example.'

They had both laughed. It had been a lovely moment of togetherness, Rayanne remembered later that day.

'I wonder what the mother would have to say,' she had said.

'In this day and age, talking about liberation and all that tripe, they might welcome it.'

'All that tripe?' Rayanne had repeated slowly, as she felt angry. What right had he to dismiss . . .? 'Look, why shouldn't a woman be treated as an equal of man?'

'Because she isn't.' He chuckled. 'All right, all right! She's as tough as a man, as intelligent as a man, but can't you stupid idiots see that as you are, you have far more control of us unfortunate males than you ever would if you were equal? What an idiotic word that is! Tell me, what do you want in this equality business?'

'The same wages, the same opportunities, the same respect . . .'

'Hey, look! That should interest you,' Cary had said, abruptly changing his voice, grabbing her arm as he slowed up the Land Rover and pointed at two warthogs who were running down the road ahead of them, having just dived out from under the bushes. They kept turning their heads anxiously, but never seemed to think of leaving the road. 'Look at their stiff little tails,' Cary said, laughing. 'Aren't they amusing?'

The interruption seemed to have closed their conversation, much to Rayanne's relief, and after a sandwich lunch with one of the bachelor wardens they went for an even longer drive round the Reserve during which she saw the lions sleeping while the lionesses prowled around, and she saw the hippos in deep water, and the blue wildebeest gathering at the drinking places.

'See what a pattern of protective orderliness there is,' Cary had said. 'Look how the young animals place themselves between the older ones. See . . . some of them drink while others keep watch and the way they sniff the air. They can smell danger.'

Finally he drove her back to the Crisps' house.

'I hope you're not too tired,' he said politely as he walked round to her side of the Land

41

Rover. He had to help her out, much to her annoyance, but, sitting on her feet, she had got caught up with a slit in the seat cover.

His voice had changed again. Gone was the relaxed friendly voice. Now he was Mr Jefferson, owner and boss of the Reserve.

'No, I'm fine. Thanks,' she said, embarrassed as he half-lifted her down. 'Thanks for showing me everything. It was most interesting.'

'Good. I'll send you round a Land Rover in the morning and a Ranger. Then you can go and look for yourself. You brought your camera, of course . . .?' He saw the hesitation in her face, for, though she had brought a camera, it was only a small one. 'Let me know if you need one. We have plenty available. Goodbye.' He shook her hand solemnly, lifted his hand in greeting to Samantha Crisp, who was standing on the *stoep* and drove away.

Samantha smiled. 'Well?' she asked. 'Bored to tears?'

'Actually,' Rayanne admitted, 'it was much more interesting than I expected it to be.'

'That's only because *he* told you about it all,' Samantha said, and laughed, clapping her hands as she watched Rayanne blush. 'Don't tell me you've fallen for him, too. Oh me, oh my . . . we poor women! Don't dream, Rayanne . . there isn't a hope.'

'I'm not dreaming,' Rayanne said stiffly, but knew her red cheeks might have given away

42

her secret. 'Actually it's simply that he's very good-looking, attractive and interesting to talk to. I've never met a man like him before.'

'And never will again,' Samantha prophesied. 'Better have a bath, if you can bear that ghastly brown water, and then come up for a drink. You must be caked with dust.'

'I must look a sight,' Rayanne admitted, laughing ruefully. 'By the way, I met Sister Macintyre and Miss Horlock.'

Samantha whistled softly. 'And how did you get on?'

Rayanne laughed. 'We didn't. Obviously Sister Macintyre didn't like the look of me, but Miss Horlock was a little more friendly. They're both very . . .'

'Dishy? You bet they are. Deliberately dishy. Silly clots! They ought to know that Cary will never marry. He's married to his work and that's all that counts . . . but they go on hoping, go on trying. It's pathetic, that's what it is. Pathetic. Now hurry and get washed up. I've cooked a good dinner for us all.'

Rayanne obeyed, shuddering as she slid into the muddy water but enjoying it all the same; grateful for the drinking water with which she washed her face and cleaned her teeth. She put on a green trouser suit and made her way to the house. Mike had promised to refill her torch with batteries, apologising profusely for not having checked the night before.

It was so peaceful sitting on the mosquito-screened *stoep*. Samantha seemed delighted to have an audience and talked most of the time. She did ask a lot of questions, though, about England, and Rayanne remembered what Cary had said.

'I think I could be happy here,' Rayanne said slowly. 'It's so quiet, so relaxed . . .'

'And so unutterably dull,' Samantha added.

Mike Crisp joined them and asked Rayanne how she had enjoyed the day. They talked of animals and soil conservation and the importance of water, and poor Samantha looked bored to tears.

It was after dinner as they were sitting on the *stoep,* a starry-skied black night outside with an occasional howl or bark to break the quietness, when the car arrived. It was not a Land Rover but a huge Jaguar.

'Oh no!' Samantha half groaned. 'It can only be . . .'

Mike had already gone down to meet the visitors. Rayanne stared at the small plump little woman with snow-white hair who came up the pathway, leaning on Cary's arm. She smiled at Rayanne as they reached the house.

'My dear child!' she said, holding out her hands. 'I'm so delighted to meet you. Any relation of my darling Joe is welcome.'

'I'm not really a relation,' Rayanne said quickly. 'His goddaughter.'

'What's the difference?' Mrs Jefferson laughed happily. 'He never married for

44

years, you know. That was because of me.' She turned to the silent Cary and tapped him on the shoulder. 'I chose your father, Cary darling. He wasn't so rich, but he was a darling. Like you,' she added, and smiled, then turned to Samantha. 'You'll forgive me if I take your guest away, won't you, Samantha? I can't bear to think of Joe's goddaughter in one of those ghastly rondavels. I told Cary so, didn't I, darling?' She smiled at him lovingly. 'As soon as he came home, I was really cross, wasn't I? Rayanne must come and stay with us, I said, and your bedroom is all ready for you, dear child. I am so happy to see you . . . it is wonderful . . .'

'It might be an idea if Miss Briscoe was to go to her rondavel and pack her things, then come back here. I'm sure Samantha will make us a cup of coffee,' Cary Jefferson said quietly.

His mother beamed. 'A wonderful idea, darling. I always enjoy Samantha's coffee.'

'I'll go with Miss Briscoe,' said Cary, taking a torch from his pocket. 'Come along.'

They walked down the narrow path, Cary striding ahead, Rayanne not sure if she was pleased or not. Living in the same house with Cary? Sitting at the same table at meals? Seeing him so much? Would she be able to hide her secret? Or wake up from the idiotic idea that she was in love with him? How could you love a man you've only known one and a quarter days? she asked herself.

45

At the rondavel, Cary waited patiently while she packed. As she straightened, he smiled at her.

'I must warn you of two things, Ray. Mother has always wanted a daughter, so you'll be smothered, or rather mother-smothered, with love. I hope it won't be a nuisance, because it'll make her happy. Secondly, don't be embarrassed if she matchmakes. Mother is convinced it's time I got married and had at least four children, if not more. She's a frustrated grandmother, you see. Mind, she's very choosy. She may take a little while to decide if you're good enough for me.'

'Well!' Rayanne felt about to explode. Of all the nerve . . .! and then Cary laughed.

'Don't let it embarrass you. I'm certain she'll find you ideal for me and do her best to throw us together in romantic situations.' He chuckled. 'You know, soft lights and sweet music that her generation used to go in for so much. So don't let it worry you. You're quite safe as far as I'm concerned.'

Rayanne stared at him. She couldn't speak. How dared he talk to her like that! If he knew the truth . . . but he must never know it, that was for sure!

She managed a light laugh. 'What a joke! I certainly wouldn't want to marry you if you were the last man on earth.'

'Is that so?' he asked, and the amusement had left his voice. 'Very interesting,' he added

46

sarcastically. 'We'd better get going or poor Samantha will begin to scream. She and Mother don't get on.'

He led the way and she watched his back and hated him one moment and knew the next that she could never really hate him. But why did he have to be so nice and then so beastly? Saying she was safe as far as he was concerned! Indeed, the arrogance of it. And then the sarcastic way he had said *'Is that so? Very interesting.'* What did he mean? Didn't he believe her? Did he, like Samantha, think she had come there for one reason? And one reason only? she asked herself. Him!

Maybe if she had known him before . . . if they had been old friends . . . but how could you chase a man you had never met? A man you had no desire to meet. But now . . . but now?

Mrs Jefferson was waiting for them and soon all were in the car, Cary driving. Back at the house, it was ablaze with lights. Mrs Jefferson fussed happily as she led Rayanne to her bedroom.

'You have your own bathroom and loo, dear child, and plenty of hot water. Do you like a big or a light breakfast? In bed?'

It was a beautiful room, Rayanne thought when she was finally alone and could look around her. She stared out of the picture window at the black night with a dark sky brightened by a beautiful new moon and stars all sparkling. The trees were silhouetted against the sky. Everything was quiet. They were high above the crocodiles and the electric light wouldn't go out . . .

Lying in bed, Rayanne relived the day, going over her conversations with Cary, wishing the talks were still to be said, for she had enjoyed the day so much. But would he ever be like that again? she wondered.

Sleepily she lay with just a sheet on her. The room had air-conditioning, so the intense humid heat of the rondavel no longer roasted her. The quick bath she had had had been lovely, too, the water clear and free of mud. She wondered how they had managed it. She had said she would get up for breakfast, but now she regretted it. She was afraid to see too much of Cary, afraid he might see in her eyes the love she could not understand. For how can you love a man you've only just met? she asked herself, and yawned. She yawned again and then fell asleep.

*   *   *

Rayanne need not have worried, for after she was called with a cup of tea, had showered, and then went to join her hostess for breakfast, Cary was not there. Mrs Jefferson beamed at her.

'So nice to have a companion for meals, my dear. I get tired of sitting alone. That's why I'm always trotting off to stay with friends.'

'Doesn't . . .' Rayanne paused. She had not yet called Cary Jefferson *Cary*, yet she could hardly call him *Mr Jefferson* to his mother. 'Your son . . .?'

'He rarely eats meals with me. He has his own flat at the other end of the house. You see, he's always out somewhere. We used to fight because he never came in at the right time for meals and I got tired of waiting for him, and he didn't like it because I had waited, so I suggested he had his own little flat, his own cook and so on.' She paused, breathless. 'When I know he's going to be in the house at a reasonable time then I invite him to dinner and we enjoy each other's company. The trouble with poor Cary is . . .' Mrs Jefferson added sadly as she helped Rayanne to kidneys and bacon . . . 'is that he's allowed his work to get control of him. He eats, sleeps and drinks conservation. He used to be so different, gay and social-minded, but that was when he was a stockbroker. He did very well. His father and I were proud of him.' She sat down opposite Rayanne and smiled. 'Am I boring you, my dear?'

'Of course not,' Rayanne said instantly. Please go on.'

'Well, my husband died and Cary told me that he had always wanted to have his own wild life reserve. You can imagine how amazed I was. He had never said anything of the sort to

49

his father or to me. I knew he enjoyed coming to the Reserves—he spent all his holidays there if we let him—but for a future! Not that I was worried about money. His father left us both very comfortably off and I knew Cary had been earning good money and had saved a lot of it. But it was the thought of living so far from civilisation—in the midst of wild animals.' She laughed and passed the marmalade to Rayanne. 'You're sure you wouldn't like some more kidneys and bacon.'

'Quite sure, thank you. You don't mind living here?'

'Mind?' Mrs Jefferson chuckled. 'I hated it at first, but I saw what it meant to Cary, so I put up with it. He's often away for weeks at a time and then I do miss him, so I usually go and stay with friends or invite them here. They find it very exciting. Frankly, it all rather bores me. It seems an awful waste of money to me to bother to keep wild animals when there are so many human beings who are starving to death.' She sighed. But there it is, my dear. When you love someone, you accept the fact that their beliefs are almost certain to be different from your own. All I want is for Cary to be happy.'

'It's a very lovely house,' Rayanne said slowly, looking round the lofty room with its walnut furniture and beautiful silver.

'It is, isn't it, my dear? Cary is so thoughtful. He knew how important a beautiful home is to me, so he had it built specially for me. He knows I like entertaining, so there are several guest rooms. It's quite a lonely life, sometimes, though, for when the courses start, I hardly see him at all.'

'The courses?'

'Yes, my dear. We have groups of students who come here for several months to have lectures and see for themselves. Cary feels strongly about this, because he wants more young people to be interested in conservation of wild life. Next week, our next course starts. It can be quite noisy. Young people of today do like such loud music, don't they?' She laughed. 'My dear child, I forgot you were one of the young people.'

'I don't like loud music, either,' Rayanne said with a smile.

A tall African in an immaculately cut khaki safari suit came in and spoke to Mrs Jefferson.

'Thank you, Kwido,' she said, and turned to Rayanne. 'Your Land Rover is at the door and Kwido will escort you. He's a well-trained mechanic and a good shot, so you'll be in safe hands. I made sure of that. I talked to Cary last night after you went to bed. I said any relation of Joe's must be treated as a V.I.P. He was a darling. I've so much to talk to you about, but of course your work must come first.' She stood up. 'Kwido will bring you back for lunch and then we can have a long talk. See you later!' Mrs Jefferson gave her a smile and left the room.

51

Rayanne went back to her own bedroom and hunted out a notebook and pencil, also her camera. She put on her blue jeans and dark shirt, remembering what Cary had said about 'publicity' attracting the monkeys. What was she going to look for? she wondered. Where should she go?

Kwido was standing by the Land Rover. He lifted his hand in greeting and she lifted hers.

'You wish to drive, madam?' he asked politely.

Rayanne shook her head quickly. She had never dared to try to learn how to drive a car. What a gorgeous source for teasing that would have made! She could just hear her brothers joking about it, and if, by sheer bad luck, she had scraped the car or had an accident, they would never have let her forget it!

'I can't drive,' she said simply.

Kwido opened the door of the Land Rover on her side. Waited while she got in, took his rifle from the back of the truck and put it by his side in front. He smiled, his white teeth bright in his dark face.

'We will not need it,' he said, and it sounded like a promise. 'Shall I just take you everywhere? Or is it one kind you want?'

'Everywhere, please, Kwido.' She moistened her dry mouth. If only she knew what she was looking for! Coming out here, though it seemed a bright idea at the time when Uncle Joe had suggested it, had not helped. 'I just

52

want to look around.'

Kwido seemed to understand. He drove carefully and took her to the different water dams and parked the Land Rover behind huge shrubs so that they could watch the animals unseen. He showed her chameleons. Kwido seemed to know a lot. He told her how when the chameleon grows old and grey it climbs on to a green twig and is young again.

'It is sad we cannot do that,' Kwido said politely, but with a smile.

Rayanne had to laugh. She made a note of what he had said. Then he showed her how the chameleon moves slowly, about an inch at a time. Its long sticky tongue shoots out to take its prey and of course it changes colour according to where it is.

There were many amusing little things Kwido told her to add to her notes. That the lioness is very vicious when she has a cub. Rayanne saw large herds of buffaloes who, Kwido told her, prefer to graze in large herds, but he also showed her how the blue wildebeest and zebra can mix with impalas as well and also baboons quite happily.

Baboons fascinated her. She made a note to ask Kwido another time to find her some place where she could watch them, for he had already told her they have their own beauty saloons, 'As in big cities,' Kwido had said, 'where they clean their young.'

Kwido took her back in good time for lunch.

It had been a hot close morning with small insects flying in her face, and about two pages of notes! Rayanne showered and changed into a white cotton frock. Uncle Joe had waned her it could be very hot, so she had made several very thin frocks, finding it impossible to buy really thin ones in wintry England.

'Well, my dear, learned a lot?' Mrs Jefferson greeted her happily. 'Cary is coming to lunch. He wants to know how you got on.'

Rayanne knew dismay instantly. Suppose he asked to see her notes? Somehow or other she must decide what she was going to write about. Perhaps his suggestion of gestation and parenthood was the best. If he realised she had no real idea what she wanted to study, he might imagine she was here to chase him!

She was welcomed warmly by Mrs Jefferson, who insisted that they sat on the *stoep* and had a refreshingly cold drink before they ate.

'Well, my dear?' she asked eagerly. 'How did you get on?'

Rayanne stretched herself luxuriously on the long low chair. 'It was most interesting.'

'And Kwido?'

'Very helpful. It was most amusing about the chameleon . . .' Rayanne told her hostess what Kwido had said. They both laughed.

'My dear child, how delectable! The perfect joke for a dinner party. I must remember it. Did you know your Uncle Joe well? I mean, do you? What is he like now? Of course he's

54

much older . . . .' Mrs Jefferson's voice was wistful.

'He's very handsome still,' Rayanne could say, and saw the beam on Mrs Jefferson's face. 'He mentioned you.'

'He did?' The old lady leaned forward, her eyes bright. 'He really did?'

Rayanne was glad she could tell the truth, for Cary had told her she was a bad liar. 'I remember he said that Cary's mother had been the most beautiful girl he had ever known.'

'He really said that?' Mrs Jefferson's day was certainly made. She leaned back in her chair, waving a little fan before her flushed face. 'He was a darling. His wife?' Her voice changed. 'I gather she is an invalid.'

'I'm afraid so. She never leaves her house. They live in Gloucester, but he often comes down to see Dad.'

'You like him? Uncle Joe, I mean?' Mrs Jefferson asked.

Rayanne hesitated. 'Yes, I've always liked him very much, but . . . well, it isn't awfully easy to talk to him. He's reserved.'

'Shy! He always was, poor darling.'

'Also I always saw him with Dad and my brothers, and that . . .' Rayanne paused, remembering Cary's accusation that she was being ultra-sensitive about her brothers. But he was wrong and she was right, she was sure of that! 'They always teased me, called me Little Girl, and wondered what had happened to my brains as they said I had none.'

Mrs Jefferson, to Rayanne's surprise, burst into laughter, dropping her fan, clapping her hands excitedly.

'My dear, he hasn't changed at all. That's exactly what he used to say to me, and I would get very angry and then I'd see the twinkle in his eyes and I'd know he was teasing me.'

'You mean he said you had no brains?' Rayanne said slowly.

My dear child, men are all the same. They have to boost their own unsteady egos and they do that by teasing us. You must never let them see you mind. That's fatal, because it'll get worse and worse.'

'It has,' said Rayanne, her voice sad.

Mrs Jefferson leant forward. 'Then don't let it, dear child. Remember that as women we are far superior to men, bless their dear hearts, and they know it and resent it. If they tease you, smile sarcastically and say something like: "Look who's talking!" or even more corny, "People in glasshouses . . ." and then laugh and walk away as if no longer interested in them.'

'And it works?'

'Certainly it works. Or it did over fifty years ago. Don't let them see you mind, whatever happens.'

'I lose my temper.'

Mrs Jefferson laughed. 'I used to, but in the end I felt sorry for them. I knew I was superior really; if it made them happier to think they were, well, why not? I lost nothing and they gained a lot.'

'I'll try . . .' Rayanne said slowly, leaning forward to watch something move on the sand banks that lined the turgid brown river. 'You don't mind having crocodiles at the bottom of your garden?'

Mrs Jefferson chuckled. 'Of course I don't. They're hideously frightening things, but I never go close to the water. It isn't their fault they look like that, is it? So I can't see that it's really fair to hate them, because they can't help acting that way. Besides, it's a lovely conversation-starter. People just stare at me as if I'm mad.'

'It's a beautiful garden . . .'

'Yes, I love it.'

A shadow crossed them. Rayanne looked up. It was Cary.

'Gossiping as usual,' he said, sitting down. 'You sound like a couple of mynah birds.'

'We were talk . . .' Rayanne began indignantly, caught Mrs Jefferson's eyes, and smiled. 'Is that a compliment or an insult, Cary?'

He looked startled. Was it because this was the first time she had called him Cary? she wondered. Or because she had smiled when he teased her?

'A compliment, of course. I brought Cary up to be polite to young ladies,' said Mrs

Jefferson. She looked at her son. 'Cary, I told you I wanted the hedge between us and Jefferson Hall tidied up. You've done nothing about it, and it looks awful.'

'You're right, it does. I'm afraid I forgot,' Cary said meekly. 'I'm sorry. I'll arrange it this afternoon. How did you get on this morning, Ray?'

'Fine, just fine.'

'She found it most interesting,' Mrs Jefferson joined in eagerly. 'She liked Kwido, too, found him very helpful.'

'Yes, he's good. I'm thinking of sending him over to the U.S.A. to do a course on conservation of soil and water. They're doing some interesting experiments there that might help us.'

'He seems to know an awful lot already,' Rayanne began, and stopped abruptly, for Cary was smiling.

'How right you are, Ray, but there's much more for him to learn. Later I hope to start another reserve of a different nature, and one day Kwido might be head warden. I believe in training men to take responsible positions. That's a sign of genius, you know.'

His mother chuckled. 'Inherited from me, of course. Isn't lunch ready?'

At that moment a bell tinkled.

'Lunching with us, Cary?' Mrs Jefferson asked.

He smiled. 'But of course. Uncle Joe's god-
58

daughter must be given V.I.P. treatment.'

Rayanne felt the anger surge up inside her Had he got to be so beastly? She clutched the back of the chair and fought her anger, finally smiling.

'How lucky I am that Uncle Joe *is* my godfather,' she said sweetly.

CHAPTER THREE

Life was certainly different for Rayanne now she was living with Mrs Jefferson. It wasn't only the large, beautifully-furnished bedroom with the pale pink silk curtains and bedspread to match, the polished floor with large soft white rugs; nor was it the clean water in which she could shower or bathe several times a day; nor the excellent food; not even the beautiful garden where they so often sat watching the hideous crocodiles slowly submerge in the muddy water or move with their slow crawl—a frightening, almost relentless crawl—across the mud. No, it was Mrs Jefferson. She was the one who made all the difference.

When Rayanne came home, driven by Kwido after trying to make notes, to work out what she wanted to write, there would be the plump, white-haired little woman, waiting eagerly. It was a warm, delighted welcome, such a welcome as Rayanne had never known before. Mrs Jefferson liked her . . . no, even more than that, she loved her. And Rayanne was beginning to love the talkative little woman who was always laying down the law to her big son and bullying him—literally bullying him into doing what she wanted done. And there was Cary, standing so quietly, saying meekly that his mother was quite right and he shouldn't have forgotten what she had asked him to do. A different Cary, an inconsistent Cary in many ways.

It was pleasant, Rayanne found, to have someone interested in what you had been doing; someone who would ask questions eagerly and listen to your answers, someone who fussed over you, made sure you had the kind of food you liked, that you were not too tired.

One day, Rayanne found herself alone in the garden with Cary. Mrs Jefferson had murmured something and gone indoors. The amused smirk on Cary's face annoyed Rayanne.

'Your mother is a darling,' she said, and wished she hadn't, because it sounded so childishly defiant.

'I'm aware of that,' he said coolly.

'Then why don't you do what she asks you to do?' Rayanne sat up in her chair and glared at him. 'It's four days she's been asking you to have that high hedge cut and . . .'

'Asking me?' Cary sounded amused. 'You

60

mean ordering me to have it done.'

'Is that why you haven't? Because you can't take orders?' Rayanne felt her control of her anger slipping away. It was such a stupid thing to get angry about, but she hated that smug, supercilious smile he was giving. 'You meekly tell her you'll do a thing, but you've no intention of doing it, have you?'

'None at all,' he agreed, and offered her a cigarette which she refused, then lit one for himself. 'Why should I?'

'She is your mother.'

'That wasn't my fault . . .'

Rayanne slid along the seat as she tensed with fury. 'How dare you say such a horrible thing! If you knew how lucky you are to have such a wonderful mother. Why do you meekly say you'll do it when you have no intention of doing what she wants done?'

He smiled. 'She knows very well I have no intention of doing what I—to quote you— meekly agree to doing. She doesn't expect me to do it.'

'Then why does she?'

He lifted his hand to silence her. 'It's a game we play.' His voice changed, losing its amusement, becoming grave. 'I think the saddest thing about you, my little Ray, is the fact that you have no conception whatsoever of a true parent-and-child relationship. Mother and I understand one another. You see, my father was a strong authoritative man who laid down the law. Mother was always meek and biddable; she knew Dad wasn't well and mustn't be upset, so she gave way about everything, even against, as she often said, her principles. When he died and we lived together, we came to an undiscussed arrangement. We didn't need words. We understood one another. For the first time in years, Mother could throw her weight around, could boss me, order me about. So she did it, knowing full well that I would do what I thought best and certainly wouldn't do what she said if I didn't agree with her—but I always pretend to agree meekly and she knows I'm pretending, so she can say the most outrageous things . . . you haven't heard anything yet! . . . and we understand perfectly what we're both doing. Do you see?'

Rayanne stared at him. She did see, yet it was hard to believe. On the other hand, if his mother expected him to do what she said, would she still love him so much when he deliberately did the opposite? Surely, Rayanne thought, then it makes sense?

'You're very lucky,' she said, moving to stand up and sliding with a bump on to the grass. She must have caught her sandal in something.

'Clumsy!' he teased as he stood up quickly, bending to take her hands in his and pull her to her feet.

Her cheeks red, she thanked him.

'My pleasure,' he told her, his eyes amused.

'Well . . .' she began, then stopped, for he was still holding both her hands tightly, looking down at her, his eyes thoughtful. 'Well . . .'

'Ray,' he said slowly, 'have you no understanding like that with your mother?'

She shook her head. 'I'm afraid we don't . . . well, in a way we do, but you see, she's so busy running round looking after Dad and . . .'

'Your five brothers. How it irks you, doesn't it? It seems sad. Most girls would be delighted to have five older brothers.'

'I'm not most girls.' She heard the defiant note creeping back in her voice. If only he would let go of her hands, she thought, and then knew that that was not what she really wanted, for she loved the touch of his fingers as they curled round hers.

'That,' he said drily, 'is obvious. I wonder what started you feeling this animosity towards your brothers. Can you remember when it began?'

Rayanne stared up at him. It was absurd, she knew, and she kept telling herself it though it had no effect on her feelings, but just to feel his hands round hers, just to be so near, made it hard to think.

'I'm ten years younger than my youngest brother . . . when I was little I always wanted to play with him, but he'd have nothing to do with me. Then I hated it when he had his first

63

girl-friend, because he was *my* brother . . . and suddenly he wasn't. Then at school—well, I wasn't very bright and . . .' She paused as his dark tufty eyebrows lifted.

'You must have been pretty bright,' he said, 'to get where you are.'

Again her cheeks burned. 'I had to work hard and just scraped through my exams. All my brothers got Honours and hardly had to work. They were just naturals, like Dad.'

'You're like your mother?'

Rayanne nodded. 'Yes, except that she's lovely. She's tall and slender with high cheekbones and gorgeous red hair. She looks absurdly young and never seems to grow old.'

'But she has no brains?'

'That's what my father says, but I think he's wrong. Mother helped me a lot with my studies.'

'Your father didn't?'

'He was always too busy with the boys. He's a lawyer, you see, and so are my brothers and . . .'

'Your father wanted you to be one?'

Rayanne shrugged. 'I don't think he thought for a moment that I could be one, but definitely he'd have liked it. He wanted to be proud of me, as he is of the others, but I let him down.'

'Ray, you're so wrong,' Cary began, then dropped her hands quickly, as if they had burned him or even stung him. Mrs Jefferson came out to join them, but if Cary had let go of Rayanne's hands because of that, then he had left it too late for his mother had a happy, almost triumphant look on her face as she beamed on them both.

'You'll be home the day after tomorrow, Cary,' said Mrs Jefferson. She didn't ask. 'I'm giving a little dinner party for Rayanne. I thought we'd ask those two nice vets, what are their names? Leslie Van der Mer and Loftus Jones? And Sister Macintyre and Christine Horlock. I haven't asked them over for some time and they must think it very rude of me.'

Cary nodded. 'That's fine, Mother.' He looked at Rayanne and his eyes were twinkling. 'This time I won't forget.' Then he left them.

Rayanne sat down and Mrs Jefferson followed suit. They sat in silence, Rayanne knowing that her companion was bursting with things that mustn't be said, questions that shouldn't be asked.

'It's a lovely day,' Rayanne said to overcome the awkward silence.

'Is it?' Mrs Jefferson looked vague and then smiled. 'Yes, dear child, I can see it is.' She positively beamed and Rayanne felt herself blushing, for she saw that Cary's mother had completely misinterpreted Rayanne's words. Mrs Jefferson thought it was a *lovely day* for Rayanne because Cary, her wonderful son, had been holding Rayanne's hands!

And wasn't it? that mocking little voice that so often hides inside us asked. Wasn't it a lovely day?

'You have met Daphne and Christine?' Mrs Jefferson asked. 'Both of them are crazy about poor Cary and chase him to death. They must be mad.'

'They're both very attractive.' As usual, Rayanne found herself leaping to the defence of anyone criticised.

'Good looks!' Mrs Jefferson said scornfully. 'Comes out of pots. But they're most unsuitable for Cary. Daphne is so bossy and she just can't talk about anything, anything at all. As for Christine . . . all she thinks about is her microscope. She isn't a bit interested in the animals, you know, and Cary thinks the world of them.' There was a little silence and then Mrs Jefferson turned to smile at Rayanne. 'I'm so glad, dear child, that you and Cary get on so well together. You're perfectly matched.'

Rayanne was looking at the little old lady and saw beyond her Cary standing in the open doorway, a huge grin splitting his handsome face. He must have heard every word his mother had just said. Rayanne couldn't resist it.

'I certainly find him very attractive, but . . . but actually we're very different, Mrs Jefferson. I find him far too arrogant.'

'Arrogant?' Mrs Jefferson sounded shocked. 'He doesn't mean to be, I'm sure. It's just that

66

he has such a responsible job and has to give orders.'

'I'm not accustomed to obeying them.'

Mrs Jefferson chuckled. 'That's the whole point, dear child. Just pretend to and go your own sweet way. I always do. It works well and makes life more fun.'

Rayanne, staring over Mrs Jefferson's shoulder, saw Cary lift his hand as if in final salute and then he walked away. She felt her tense body relax.

'You're being very kind to me,' Rayanne said, deliberately changing the subject. 'I'm so grateful.'

Mrs Jefferson leant forward and patted Rayanne's knee.

'Don't thank me, dear child, I love having you here. I've always wanted a daughter— someone like you. I don't think I've ever felt so optimistic about the future before.'

Again Rayanne felt her cheeks go hot. If only Cary's mother would stop planning the impossible. Rayanne was certain that Cary didn't see her as a *woman* . . . a woman he could love. Indeed, she wondered if he saw any women as people he could love; most of them seemed to be 'headaches'.

'Do you dress up when you give dinner parties?' she asked, more as a ruse to guide Mrs Jefferson's thoughts away from her son's possible marriage. 'I don't think I expected anything like that. I thought this would be purely a working holiday.'

'Let's have a look at your wardrobe.' Mrs Jefferson stood up and then paused. 'Is that impertinent? I mean, I didn't mean . . .'

Rayanne smiled. 'Of course I know you didn't, and I don't mind in the least showing you.'

They walked down the *stoep* to Rayanne's door, which was never locked. Inside, Rayanne showed Mrs Jefferson the few cocktail party dresses she had.

'Do the others dress up?' she asked.

The plump little woman chuckled. 'And how! It's a positive battle, Rayanne dear. It's very funny, but also very sad. I wonder.' She stood back, looking at Rayanne's figure. 'I wonder . . . Just wait a moment. I'll be back.'

Rayanne nodded and hung up her black trouser suit that was far too hot for this climate. Her green sparkling dress—that was also too hot. The evenings were so humid that anything but the thinnest dresses clung to your damp skin.

Mrs Jefferson came hurrying back; hanging over her arm was a pale blue satin dress. She shook it out and held it up before her. It came to the ground and had frills on the short sleeves and a high waistline, embroidered and smocked.

'It's beautiful . . .!' Rayanne exclaimed.

'Try it on, try it on,' Mrs Jefferson told her excitedly. 'I can't wait to see it on you.'

Rayanne slipped out of her yellow cotton frock and carefully put on the soft satin one. It fitted her perfectly. She looked in the glass.

'It's absolutely fabulous!' she said slowly. 'But how did you know my size?'

She saw Mrs Jefferson's reflection in the mirror. The little old lady was shaking with laughter, unable to speak. Rayanne swung round. 'What's the joke?'

'Oh dear . . oh dear me . . . I'm sorry, Rayanne dear, but I can't stop laughing.' Slowly she gained control, then wiped her tearful eyes and smiled.

'It was my nightie, Rayanne—my trousseau nightie. My mother gave it to me. She said the colour was romantic. I never wore it—Cary's father loathed pale blue. He had a passion for white underclothes, as we called them in those days.' She chuckled. 'You look beautiful in it. Of course, I was much thinner in those days. I couldn't get into it now.'

'I can borrow it?' Rayanne was looking in the mirror again. The colour certainly did something to her. It was just too beautiful for words and absolutely *fashionable*.

Mrs Jefferson laughed. 'No, you may not borrow it, dear child, but I'm giving it to you. It's lain all these years in a drawer, it must be bored to tears, poor thing. It's far too beautiful to be hidden away, so please let me make it a gift.'

Rayanne caught her breath and stared

at the happy, beaming little woman. 'It's wonderful of you!' Impulsively she hugged the older woman, kissing her. 'You're such a darling!'

'I'm . . . I'm glad you think . . . think so,' Mrs Jefferson almost stammered, her eyes suddenly filled with tears. She turned and hurried out of the room, leaving Rayanne puzzled, but she soon forgot the generous little old lady, as she gently stroked the satin and turned round, gazing in the mirror. It really did things to her.

*　　　*　　　*

As the time for the dinner party grew near Rayanne's self-confidence diminished. The beautiful pale blue satin dress delighted her, of course, but she wasn't happy with her hair. She had washed it—as she did every few days, for the dust from her Land Rover trips with Kwido was dreadful—but today it seemed limp and without life. Carefully she made up. If only she was beautiful, she thought, leaning forward, gazing in the mirror as she carefully applied her eyelashes. If only she was tall and slim, with long lovely legs, and high cheekbones and her mother's red hair! If only . . .

What good would it do? she asked herself cynically. As if it would help matters! Cary, the only person who really mattered in her life, wouldn't notice any difference if she

70

suddenly became beautiful, that was for sure. Cary wouldn't notice anything about her, she thought miserably.

Yet, later that evening, it seemed that she was wrong. She had been waiting with Mrs Jefferson for the visitors. The little old lady wore a scintillating pale pink voile gown, decorated with sparkling beads. Her white hair was piled high, her cheeks slightly flushed, her eyes shining.

'We'll show them, Rayanne my dear,' she said, holding Rayanne's hand for a moment. 'We'll show them,' she repeated triumphantly.

Rayanne wondered what she meant, but at that moment the visitors arrived.

Christine Horlock was first. The tall blonde with her lovely face and blue eyes was wearing a long black dress, slit on either side to show her beautiful long legs. She wore a long necklace, three times twisted round her throat, of sparkling gems.

'Mrs Jefferson, how well you're looking. This is very kind of you,' she said in her attractive voice. She glanced at Rayanne. 'Hullo,' she said casually. 'You're looking very smart today,' she added, her voice amused.

Rayanne blushed, remembering what she must have looked like when they met before.

'She looks beautiful, doesn't she?' Mrs Jefferson said quickly. 'I think that is her colour, don't you?'

'It's very beautiful,' Christine agreed.

71

Then came Sister Daphne Macintyre, equally lovely in a different way; tall, slim, with dark hair, lovely dark eyes and that magically attractive husky voice.

'Mrs Jefferson, I can see your holiday did you the world of good. You look so well!'

'You have met Rayanne?' Mrs Jefferson said with a smile.

It was strange, but Daphne Macintyre's face seemed to change, Rayanne noticed. It hardened, yet she smiled, a smile that didn't reach her eyes. 'Yes, I have met Miss Briscoe. How is your work going?' she asked. 'Or isn't it?' she added.

'Very well indeed,' said Mrs Jefferson, giving Rayanne no time to speak. 'Too fast for my liking, because I would like Rayanne to stay for ever.'

Then the two vets came with Cary. Rayanne hardly noticed the two men, Leslie someone or other, a tall, broad-shouldered man with dark hair and a short pointed beard, and Loftus Jones, a little man with sandy hair and freckles all over his face, for she was looking at Cary.

And then Rayanne's face flamed with embarrassment as Mrs Jefferson said: 'Doesn't Rayanne look beautiful, Cary dear? I really think this dress was made for her.'

Cary looked grave. 'I agree, Mother. The colour is perfect and the style very fashionable. You look very beautiful, Ray,' he said almost solemnly.

72

Rayanne wanted to run and hide, or the floor to open and swallow her. Never in all her life had she felt so embarrassed. She could see the quick amused glance Christine and Daphne had exchanged and the way the two vets were staring at her.

'Your mother gave me the frock,' Rayanne said, then wished she hadn't, for perhaps Cary had seen it before, perhaps he knew it was his mother's 'wedding nightie'; he might even, with his strange sense of humour, make a joke about it.

Fortunately Mrs Jefferson took charge of the situation.

'What about a nice cold drink for us all, Cary dear? You're the host. Your poor old mother shouldn't have to remind you . . .'

He smiled, bent and kissed her. 'My poor old mother enjoys doing so. What'll you all have?' He led the way to the small but beautiful little bar, made of woven straw.

They followed him, Loftus and Leslie walking with Daphne and Christine, Rayanne with her hostess.

As they sat on the *stoep,* drinking and talking, Mrs Jefferson constantly drew Cary's attention to Rayanne. Not that he seemed to mind. He sat next to her and began talking about a baby giraffe that had been born that morning.

'I had meant to tell you so that you could come and witness it, but the giraffe fooled us all, for we hadn't expected the little one for another week. Tell Kwido to take you there in the morning,' he said.

'Thank you. I'd love to see it,' said Rayanne, very conscious that though Christine and Daphne were joking and laughing with the two men who were including Mrs Jefferson into the conversation, both Christine and Daphne kept looking her way, both had eyes that were watching her, suspiciously. Did they think she was playing up to Cary's mother in the hope of getting Cary? Rayanne wondered. If so, they must be mad. . Absolutely mad!

At dinner, Rayanne sat next to Cary. This, of course, was his mother's doing! In fact all through the meal, it was embarrassing, for Mrs Jefferson constantly said things that implied that something exciting and wonderful might soon be announced.

Later when the ladies went out to the *stoep* and the men stayed behind for their port, Daphne Macintyre sat down next to Rayanne.

'How are things going?' she asked bluntly. 'You seem to have won over the old girl.'

'I don't understand . . .' Rayanne began, hastily standing up, not telling the truth.

Daphne laughed. An ugly laugh, very different from her usual attractively husky voice. 'Oh, don't be so dumb. You know very well what I mean. Is Sir Joe Letherington really your godfather?'

Rayanne's quick temper flared. 'Of course

74

he is,' she said angrily. 'I'm not a liar, nor,' she added, 'am I interested in Cary Jefferson. You can have him if you want him . . . that is, of course, if you can get him.' She turned away and bumped into someone.

Startled as she felt warm firm hands on her arms steadying her, she looked up, and found herself gazing closely into Cary's face. How quietly he must have come up! How much had he heard?

Now he took her arm. 'I want to show you something, Ray. We won't be a moment, Mother,' he apologised as they passed the plump little old lady, holding court with Loftus Jones, who was laughing at something she said.

Mrs Jefferson beamed, That's all right, darling. Take your time.'

Rayanne almost ran out of the room, but Cary's hand held her back. He took her to a room she had never been in before, obviously his study—a small high-ceilinged room lined with books with a desk close to the window. He closed the door behind him and leaned against it, releasing her arm.

She turned to stare at him. 'You have something to show me?'

He smiled. 'Only myself.'

Rayanne frowned, puzzled. Was he joking? If so . . .

He moved towards her so that they stood close together, but he did not touch her. He looked down at her.

'First I want to apologise.'

'Apologise?' she echoed.

'Yes, for my mother's behaviour. She's so frightened I'll fall for the wrong kind of person that she'll go to any lengths. She has decided that you would make me a suitable wife, so . . .'

'So?' Rayanne lifted her chin. 'So what?'

'So she's determined to show Christine and Daphne that you're the chosen one.'

'Chosen?' Rayanne asked bitterly. 'By whom?'

Cary smiled. 'By her, of course.'

There was a pause that seemed never-ending. Then Rayanne found her voice.

'Of course,' she said. 'If that's all . . .'

'It isn't.' Even as she moved, he moved, too, standing between her and the door. 'There is something else?'

'Something else?' she repeated.

'Yes. Why do you hate men? Or are you afraid of them?'

She stared at him, bewildered. 'Who ever said I hated or feared men?'

'No one. It stands out a mile. Every time a man enters the room, your whole body stiffens, your face goes hard, your eyes are full of— either fear or animosity. I can't make it out.'

'But I don't hate men . . .' Rayanne's voice rose slightly, and at that moment the door opened.

It was Christine. She looked at the two standing there and she looked amused.

'It's taken you a long time to show Miss Briscoe whatever it is you had to show her, Cary. Maybe she doesn't understand. Perhaps I could help.'

Cary laughed. 'No one can help, thanks. We'll finish this discussion another time, Ray. Okay?'

'Okay,' she said stiffly, and followed them back to the large beautiful drawing-room where the others were talking.

What had it all been about? she asked herself, as she sat by Mrs Jefferson's side, laughing at her jokes, listening and trying to hear what was being said, for all the time her mind felt confused, muddled, because nothing made sense. Why had Cary taken her out on her own simply to apologise? Or was it to annoy Christine and Daphne? Or perhaps to delight his mother? But was that fair to his mother? Rayanne found herself thinking. If his mother really wanted Cary to marry this English girl and there was no hope of him wanting to do so, then was it fair to let Mrs Jefferson think there was hope? It was all such a muddle, and it was hateful to have Christine look at her like that and Daphne's voice change when she spoke to whom she obviously saw as her *rival*. If only she could slip away quietly to bed, Rayanne thought miserably. She wasn't enjoying this at all . . .

But there was to be no escape. Mrs Jefferson said proudly:

77

'Rayanne tells me she's quite a good pianist.'

Her face bright red, Rayanne denied it. 'I didn't! I said I played by ear. I can't read a note.'

'Then you can hardly be called a pianist,' Daphne Macintyre said drily.

'Let's hear you, Ray,' Cary said quickly, going to the small spinet which stood by the wall facing the window. 'Mother sometimes plays on this, so we regularly have it tuned.'

'No, I . . .' Rayanne began, suddenly terrified, aware of critical eyes.

'But, Miss Briscoe, you must play for us,' Christine said sweetly. 'I'm longing to hear you. It fascinates me so to meet someone who plays by ear.'

Rayanne stood up reluctantly, well aware that Christine was convinced it was all a lie, that Rayanne couldn't play a note, that she had lied in boasting about it and that this would betray her! How pleased Christine and Daphne would be.

Sitting by the spinet, Rayanne stretched her fingers, looked round. 'What shall I play?' she asked.

'Whatever you can,' said Christine, a sarcastic tinge in her voice.

'Anything you like, Ray,' Cary said. 'We're waiting.'

Rayanne half-closed her eyes, trying to shut out the picture of those in the room. This had

78

always been her escape—when she had felt most forlorn, most despairing of ever being 'someone', of winning her father's approval and love—then she had fled to the piano. Just dreaming her way through the sound, letting her fingers take control, had always comforted her. Not that her family appreciated it; indeed she never played when any of them were around if she could help it, for she would only have got rude comments, teasing because she couldn't 'learn to play properly'.

Shutting out the rest of the world, Rayanne imagined herself and Cary alone on an enormous empty beach, holding hands, running, dancing along the wet sand, feeling the warm caressing touch of the incoming tide . . . her fingers touched the keys and she could see Cary laughing at her, could hear herself laughing, too. She could feel the happiness she had always dreamed of, the security his warm hand gave hers, the wonder of the knowledge that he loved her, that she was his . . . Vaguely she heard a haunting tune as her fingers explored sound.

Suddenly she stopped, opened her eyes and shook herself. It was strange. She looked round, stung by the silence. Had she made a fool of herself? she wondered.

'Ray, that was beautiful,' Cary said slowly, his voice amazed. 'Wasn't it, Mother?'

'Lovely, really lovely, Rayanne dear,' Mrs Jefferson said, her voice husky, a few tears running down her soft cheeks. 'Could you play it again?'

Rayanne shook her head. 'I'm afraid not. I never can.'

'But you must have learned it from somewhere,' Daphne said impatiently. 'You couldn't have composed it.'

'I . . hardly heard it myself. What did I play?' Rayanne asked.

Christine laughed. 'Honestly, you must have heard it! It was loud enough. Triumphant . . .'

'I don't agree,' said Cary, his quiet voice sounding more impressive to Rayanne than if he had shouted. 'I thought it was beautiful—a happy tune. The melody of a dream.' He looked at Rayanne. 'Am I right?'

Her cheeks flamed with embarrassment. 'Quite right, Cary,' she said with equal quietness.

CHAPTER FOUR

Next morning, Rayanne asked Kwido to take her to see the small giraffe. It was fascinating to watch the little animal with his unsteady legs. Mike Crisp was there and he told her a lot about giraffes that she had not realised.

'You can learn from a book,' Mike said scornfully, 'and know nothing. It's when you live with them that you know.'

80

Rayanne's notes were, at last, growing longer. But she still had no idea what sort of thesis she would finally write.

Kwido drove her back to the house and as she walked in on her way to her bedroom, for her usual shower and change of clothes, Rayanne paused, for Mrs Jefferson's voice was clearly audible through the half-open drawing-room door.

'Honestly, Cary, you could have spared me this. You know how I hate that girl!'

'It isn't my fault, Mother. I didn't ask her to come.'

'Then . . .'

Rayanne stood still. It was wrong to eavesdrop, she knew, and yet . . . Who were they talking about? she wondered. Could it be herself?

'You must have given her your address, Cary,' Mrs Jefferson said crossly.

'I did not, Mother,' Cary said in that maddening, exasperated, patient voice he often used. 'Without being boastful, you must admit that everyone south of the Equator—and many north of it, too—know where the Jefferson Wild Life Reserve is. I met Aileen in London at one of the conferences and have thought nothing of her since. Is it my fault if she chose to honour us with a visit? After all, Aileen Hampton is a veterinary surgeon, interested in wild life conservation, doing a tour of the world's reserves, and she does mix with the world's elite.'

'But why wait until the last moment and send you a cable? She'll be arriving this afternoon!' Mrs Jefferson almost wailed. 'I'll have to put her up here—I can't let her go into one of those ghastly rondavels.'

'Perhaps she's coming to visit you, Mother,' Cary said, again with that amused sarcastic voice Rayanne hated so much. 'After all, she met you first. That's how she introduced herself to me. She came up and said: *Cary Jefferson, I believe?* and when I confessed she was right, she went on: *I met your charming mother in Paris and she told me all about your wonderful Reserve.* You see, Mother, it was all your fault. If you didn't blow the trumpet of praise for your only son, she might never have heard of me.'

Mrs Jefferson sighed. 'Well, it's too late to do anything about it.'

Cary chuckled. 'You have to admire her for bright thinking,' he laughed as Rayanne hurried away, and added: 'That's why she sent the cable.'

In her own bedroom, Rayanne hastily showered; the cool water refreshed her hot dusty skin, and she brushed her hair vigorously. How conceited Cary was! Yet could you blame him, she asked herself, when girls so blatantly chased him? It was all a joke to him, something to laugh at. But was it as funny for the unfortunate girls who fell for his charm? On the other hand, was that *his* fault?

There was a simple solution, of course, she told her reflection in the mirror sternly as she carefully made up. She could run away! Run away as fast as she could before she got hurt still more! It was as simple as that. So why didn't she? she asked herself. She knew the answer, therefore it was a waste of time to put it into words. She loved the wretched man . . . she loved him!

She stood very still, staring at herself in the mirror, pressing her hand hard against her trembling mouth. So she would stay on as long as she could, being a fool, a stupid fool? Was that what love did to you? What would happen next? This Aileen person was almost certain to be tall and slim, with beautiful long legs and a lovely face . . .

Rayanne found it difficult to join Mrs Jefferson for lunch, but it had to be done. Rayanne was surprised when Mrs Jefferson said nothing about the new visitor; indeed, Mrs Jefferson seemed to be in a strange mood. It could hardly be called *depressed;* perhaps a more accurate word would be *thoughtful.*

So the meal passed with very little said and afterwards Rayanne pleaded an imaginary task of writing, for she had a strong feeling that Mrs Jefferson would like to be alone; that she had something important to think about.

After typing out the notes she had made— Cary had lent her a portable typewriter, scolding her for her lack of thought in not bringing one out with her—Rayanne walked in the garden. It was so hot that as she walked the perspiration trickled down her face; the glare made her eyes ache, yet she felt too restless to stay in her room. If only she had a car of her own, Rayanne thought, and added: and could drive it! It would be nice to go and see Samantha Crisp and have a chat. In Africa it was essential to have a car of your own; particularly in a backwater like this.

A backwater like this . . . she repeated the words slowly. Where had she heard them? Samantha, of course, in one of her usual moans about the loneliness. Samantha had no car, nor could she drive, either. Both Daphne Macintyre and Christine Horlock had their own cars and Rayanne gathered that they frequently drove to the small town thirty-four miles away. Out here that distance was nothing, you got there in about half an hour. Now, Rayanne was thinking, if only she had a car she could see something of Africa and its beauty . . . but what was the good, for she wouldn't be here much longer. How long could she stay? she wondered. Mrs Jefferson had begged her to stay as long as she could. That was what Rayanne wanted too, but how would Cary react?

The garden was very beautiful. She walked right down to the water's edge and shuddered as she watched a crocodile moving with his slow crawl over the sandbank, then pausing, yawning, opening his huge mouth. He looked so absorbed in what he was doing, so determined to get what he wanted. It was funny how scared she was of crocodiles, she told herself. The other animals didn't frighten her at all—except that she thought hippos and rhinos were so hideous she preferred not to look at them! Was she really so interested in wild life conservation? she asked herself. Or was it all because of Cary?

She walked back slowly towards the house. How lovely were the trees with the bougainvilleas, a lovely purple, climbing up their trunks, and those with their small white scented blossoms. This was a beautiful place. She could live here so happily.

Rayanne's mind seemed to skid to a standstill. Surely she hadn't been stupid enough to get as far as dreaming that maybe one day . . .?

'Ray!' a familiar deep voice startled her.

She turned and saw Cary striding towards her. He was wearing a safari suit and had bare legs and feet. As he came closer she saw his hair was rumpled and he looked tired. This was so unusual that she found herself saying:

'What's happened?'

He smiled ruefully. 'Nearly a tragedy. Down the river three piccanins were playing in the water—they said at the edge, but even that's dangerous. Anyhow, a croc grabbed the leg of

85

one and tried to drag the piccanin in . . . one boy hung on to his friend's arm, but the croc was winning, so the other one grabbed a stick and stuck it in the croc's eye . . . that made him let go.'

'He's all right?'

'Taken to hospital, and he may lose his leg. The one that saved him raced up to one of the wardens and shouted for help. I was there, so we went down. A bright piccanin to think of it. His father works here.'

'Then shouldn't he know not to paddle in the water?'

Cary looked amused. 'Isn't it a temptation for anyone to swim on a day as hot as this?'

'Then you find it hot, too? I thought it was just me.'

Cary laughed. 'The *rooinek* sensitive touch, eh? No, it's unusually hot. By the way, we're having a visitor.'

'We are?' Rayanne tried to sound surprised. She felt uncomfortably guilty because of what she had overheard that morning.

'Yes—a bit of a bind. She thinks she knows everything, and I can't stand that kind of woman.'

'Really?' Rayanne, remembering what his mother had said, smiled. 'Can you stand any type of woman?'

Cary put his hand under her elbow. 'Let's get some shade,' he said. 'That is a provocative question.'

86

There were several chairs and a round white table under an enormous tree, through whose branches, covered closely with dark green leaves, the sun could hardly find its way.

Cary gave her a gentle push so that she had to sit down, then he pulled up a chair and sat down opposite, narrowing his eyes as he looked at her.

'What makes you think I hate women?'

'I didn't say hate.' Rayanne lifted her hand and touched each finger as she spoke. 'I said can you stand any type of woman. First I hear you say women are a headache, then a nuisance and now a bind. Doesn't that rather imply that you would prefer to be without us?'

'Heaven forbid!' said Cary, smiling at her. 'How miserable and boring life would be if we were all men.'

'I wonder if you'd really mind. With your dedication to work, surely.'

'You've been listening to my mother! Actually I spend a lot of time enjoying my leisure. I'd say I like women very much—but in their proper place.'

'And where is that?' Rayanne paused, then smiled: 'In England it would be by the kitchen sink, of course, but as you're lucky enough to have a good staff, I suppose it's behind the coffee table.'

'In a way, yes,' Cary said slowly, as if thinking. 'On the other hand, wouldn't she be a bit of a bore? I mean, Daphne is rather

87

like that. She never reads anything, she just isn't interested in the world or its inhabitants. She's an excellent nurse . . . but let's face it, she admitted it to us once, she only became a nurse because she was told it was a good way of finding a husband.'

'But she's very beautiful. I'm sure she . . .'

'Beauty isn't everything a man wants, you know.' He offered her a cigarette and when she refused asked if she'd mind if he had one.

'Of course not. I just don't care for smoking.'

'Sensible girl.' He blew out a great puff of smoke. She felt the urge to tell him how bad it was for his lungs, but she held her tongue, because it was no business of hers! 'Well, to return . . . what sort of woman, you asked me?'

'I did not. You twist everything. I said *where is woman's proper place?*'

He smiled. 'I accept the correction meekly. Now, where is woman's proper place? Perhaps I should say in a man's arms.'

There was a silence, a silence Rayanne could almost hear as she stared at him. She shivered. Had he guessed the truth? Had he seen in her eyes that that was just where she wanted to be? In his arms.

Then Cary laughed and broke the moment up.

'I know you're not thinking that way, Ray. I think I'd like a woman to have an interest in life; perhaps voluntary work; perhaps a

88

career—something that makes her use her brains and mix with people. I like extroverts, rather than introverts—I don't like women who throw their weight around and think they know everything. Aileen Hampton is one of these. I daresay she's a good vet, but she needn't keep telling me so.' He looked up towards the house. 'Ah, she's come. Good. I'm glad I found you out here.'

'You are?' Rayanne was startled. 'But why?'

'I want her to see that I'm already bespoken.' He chuckled. 'That is, if you don't mind me using you as the dummy. I guess you're used to it by now with all Mother's ramblings. She'll bring Aileen out. Try to look at me as if you like me, Ray, and not your usual haughty look.'

'I look at you . . .' Rayanne paused. It was all happening so fast. Cary was making use of her as he believed this Aileen was chasing him! He thought it meant nothing, then . . . then he had no idea, Rayanne comforted herself, that she loved him?

He smiled and put his hand lightly round her shoulders after he pulled her to her feet. 'We'd better go and meet them.'

As they walked across the lawn, she was only really conscious of the touch of his hand on her warm arm, and then she saw the group coming out on to the *stoep* and down the few steps to the grass.

Mrs Jefferson led the way, her plump little

body in a pale yellow frock, her hands clasped in front of her waist, her face worried as she was followed by a girl and a man.

'Ah, Cary, there you are. I couldn't find you. Your guests have arrived,' she called, her voice clear in the quiet hot air.

Behind her followed the tall girl, with long slender legs, a beautiful face and red hair!

Rayanne caught her breath. Why, that was how her mother must have looked when she was young. That lovely cloud of red hair—the high cheekbones, the rather full mouth, the warm smile . . .

'Miss Hampton. I hope the drive here from the airport wasn't too exhausting,' Cary said, shaking hands. 'I want you to meet Rayanne Briscoe.'

Aileen Hampton smiled at Rayanne. A warm smile; genuine, surely, Rayanne thought.

'Cary,' Aileen turned to him, ignoring the formality in his voice, 'I do hope you'll forgive me, but I brought a friend along, Burt West.' She turned to the man by her side.

Rayanne stared at him and he stared back. There was nothing striking about him except that he was very short—about her height, she noticed. He gave her a friendly smile. His blond hair was untidy, he looked tired.

'I hope you'll forgive me, Mr Jefferson, but it was a chance in a thousand. I'm a professional photographer and would be most grateful if you'd let me take photographs of

90

what goes on here. I'm planning an article on this wild life conservation,' he said. 'It's not easy to break the barrier of Jefferson Hall,' he added, with a rather sweet shy smile, 'and when I met Aileen and she told me she was coming here and suggested I escorted her . . . well . . .' he gave a little nervous laugh, 'I took the chance. I'd show you the article and the photographs before I submitted them to the magazine, of course. I really am interested,' he added, a pleading note in his voice.

'How funny,' Rayanne said quickly, feeling sorry for him and wondering why Cary was so silent.

'I'm writing a thesis on wild life conservation.'

Burt West smiled at her almost gratefully. 'Then we're looking for the same thing.' He turned to silent Cary and smiled. 'Let's face it, I admit I've never had much time for wild life conservation and I thought if I could see it for myself and how it works out, I might understand how you chaps feel about it.'

Cary's stern face relaxed. 'How right you are! We shall try to convert you. Of course you can stay with us. I don't know if we have room in the house, but there are . . .'

Mrs Jefferson stepped forward. 'Most certainly not, Cary. No guest of mine is going into one of those rondavels. We'll be delighted to have you stay a while, Mr West.'

He smiled at her. 'Burt, please, Mrs

Jefferson. This is awfully good of you.'

'You've come at a good time,' Cary said. 'The next course starts in a few days, and you might be interested in the lectures and tours we take the students on.'

'Oh, I will be. This is marvellous.' Burt pressed his hands together and smiled at them all. 'A chance in a lifetime!'

'And how are you, Cary?' Aileen Hampton asked, moving to his side. 'You look a bit harassed.'

'Well, we've just had a kid nearly caught by a croc, and it's always rather shattering.'

'He's all right?'

Mrs Jefferson was pale. 'He wasn't . . .?'

'No.' Cary quickly told them what he had already told Rayanne.

'I hope the crocodile's eye wasn't hurt,' said Aileen. 'Is he still there?'

'No, he slid off in the water when he saw us running down. I felt like shooting him,' said Cary.

'It really does happen?' Burt said eagerly. 'I mean . . .'

'Only,' Cary's voice was curt, 'if you're fool enough to walk in the river, or near the edge.'

Burt got the message, for he grinned. 'Don't worry, I'm not a fool.'

'I think we'd better show our visitors to their rooms,' Mrs Jefferson said. 'And you, Cary, must go and wash your face. I've never seen you looking like that. And no socks or shoes—

92

tch, tch! Come along, my dear.' She took Aileen's arm. 'I hope you'll enjoy your visit here.'

'I'm sure I shall,' Aileen Hampton smiled at Cary. 'I've been looking forward to it for a long time.'

Rayanne found herself walking by Burt West's side. He yawned and grinned, 'Sorry about that. I find this heat rather exhausting. Where are you from?'

'England. And you?' Rayanne found it easy to talk to him. Maybe because she hadn't to tilt her head and look up at him? she wondered.

'London. I've known Aileen for years. A real beaut, isn't she?'

'She certainly is,' Rayanne said warmly, and knew the pangs of jealousy, for Cary was talking to the girl, laughing, his hand under her elbow as he helped her up the few steps to the *stoep*.

*　　*　　*

The next few days were strange ones for Rayanne. Sometimes she wondered if they could really be happening or if there was something wrong with herself, for nothing made sense.

In the first place, Mrs Jefferson practically ignored her. Normally this wouldn't be strange, but after the fuss she had made of Rayanne, and the real love she had shown, her sudden chilliness, her ignoring Rayanne while spending all her time talking eagerly to Aileen Hampton was so completely different that Rayanne could not help feeling hurt. Had she done something wrong? she wondered. Said something unintentionally that annoyed Mrs Jefferson—or was it just that Cary's mother had decided Aileen Hampton would be the perfect wife for Cary?

Maybe she would, for no one could deny that Aileen was one of the nicest people Rayanne had ever known. Very friendly, always paying little compliments about 'that colour matches your eyes perfectly' or 'you should wear long dresses more often, they give you a glamorous look'. Not silly, obviously false compliments, but words said with sincerity. Aileen and Rayanne spent many an hour late at night talking together, feeling the heat and sitting on the screened *stoep,* looking at the beauty of the starlit sky. They learned to know one another well. Aileen was an only child, smothered with love, while Rayanne felt that no one in her family cared for her. They discussed their problems, gave one another advice. It was impossible, Rayanne knew, that no matter how envious and jealous she felt, it was impossible not to like Aileen very much.

The only person who didn't was Cary! This was the oddest thing to Rayanne, for she just could not understand why he was so cool and impersonal to Aileen, often formal, almost rude. He rarely talked to her alone; far more often seeking out Rayanne and sitting with her.

Right from the beginning, they seemed to have divided up into strange groups. That first evening Cary had turned to Rayanne.

'Ray, would you mind taking Burt round with you and Kwido? I'm rather short of Land Rovers at the moment. Seeing you're both interested in the same phase of wild life conservation, it might help.'

'Of course I don't mind,' Ray had agreed instantly.

And so, during the mornings, sometimes in the afternoons, Rayanne and Burt would go off with Kwido. It was in many ways much more interesting, Rayanne found. She liked Burt; they were both relaxed together. Kwido showed them everything and Burt never stopped asking questions. He carried with him a small tape recorder—so that later in the afternoon he and Rayanne could listen to Kwido's descriptions, and make notes of what they felt was important.

Meanwhile Cary would take Aileen Hampton and leave her with Leslie and Loftus, saying that he was busy preparing for the next lot of students. It was true that the staff was already arriving and that no doubt Cary was busy, Rayanne thought, but she didn't feel this really excused his behaviour, for he was little short of rude to Aileen. Not that Aileen worried about it. If she and Rayanne ever discussed Cary, Aileen was full of admiration. She thought he was a wonderful man, unselfish, dedicated, a devoted son; in fact, super! That he would make some lucky woman a wonderful husband. It was obvious she was hoping to be the 'lucky woman'. Rayanne learned how to agree laughingly, to talk lightly of Christine and Daphne's attempts to 'hook him', and Aileen, having met them both during her introduction to everyone and everything, agreed that they 'hadn't a hope'.

'Cary is different. He wants someone with more than a pretty face,' Aileen said. 'He needs someone who understands his fanatic love not only for animals but for everything to do with them.'

In the evenings Rayanne would feel sorry for Aileen, though, oddly enough, Aileen didn't seem to notice anything strange, for every night Cary chose to sit by Rayanne, making it obvious that he liked her company, doing many little thoughtful things that surprised Rayanne and hurt her as well, for she knew he was doing it for one reason only. Not because he loved her—but because he wanted to make Aileen realise there was 'no hope'. Yet Aileen seemed happy enough, chatting with Mrs Jefferson and Burt; or with Leslie and Loftus, whom Mrs Jefferson frequently invited, sometimes with and sometimes without Christine and Daphne.

Then the students arrived. Most of them were in their late teens, great husky lads full of noise and laughter which would sometimes drift across the garden to the house. There were quite a few girls, all dressed in crazy-looking clothes but obviously enjoying their stay. The lectures were in the afternoons, so Rayanne and Burt were able to attend. Burt would sit, looking entranced, as he listened to Cary's lectures.

There was no doubt, Rayanne thought, but Cary was a wonderful lecturer. He could make the dullest facts interesting. He could show them the importance of conservation, the difficulties, the plans for the future. He could even prove the importance of preserving the wild life of the country.

Burt admitted he was converted. 'Somehow I hadn't thought of it that way,' he told Rayanne.

'I know, that was how I felt at first. It seemed such a waste of money to keep all these wild animals in safe comfort when so many millions of people were starving and homeless,' she agreed. 'Yet now . . .'

The students seemed really interested and there were a number of small buses which took them round the reserve every day. Of course the skill of the game catchers was demonstrated and the students saw how the animals were drugged for examination, or transported to a different reserve. Naturally the students were fascinated by the crossbow and dart that looked like an ordinary hypodermic syringe with a tail added and that when it sank into the animal's hide or skin, soon drugged him and sent him to sleep. After the examination, treatment or removal, an antidote to the drug was given and the animal recovered within seconds and without any harm having been done. In fact, frequently wounds had been treated or even operations performed successfully.

Rayanne, Burt and Kwido followed some of the demonstrations, but Cary said to them that later he would let them take part in a real one.

'I've promised to transport a dozen white hippos to England. It's going to be quite a performance.'

Rayanne said nothing, but she wondered just how long Aileen and Burt planned to stay! Which rather applied to her, too, she thought worriedly. How long could you pretend it took to write a thesis? And what was she going to write? She always had the fear that one day Cary would ask to see it. How could she refuse when he had been so generous as to let her stay for so long?

Burt was producing some amazingly good photos. He even said that maybe he would write a book about it all. He smiled as he spoke.

'Aiming high, but why not? I'm a journalist.'

'But are people sufficiently interested?'

Rayanne asked.

'We should make them,' said Burt, his freckles showing bright in the sunshine.

One evening Rayanne was late joining the 'family group' as Mrs Jefferson called it with a quick smile at Aileen, and Cary was sitting next to Aileen, listening to what she was saying, nodding his head. He looked up as Rayanne entered the room, left Aileen immediately, though she was in the middle of a sentence, and went to Rayanne, to lead her to a chair, get her a drink and sit down by her side.

Rayanne looked at him, keeping her voice very quiet. 'Is it necessary to be so rude?' she asked.

Cary smiled. 'Was it so obvious? Then it was successful. The best remedy is to behave so badly that the hunter loses interest,' he said with equal quietness, bending close to her.

Rayanne was looking at Aileen. Surely it must have hurt her? Or was she so sure of success that things like this seemed to her trivial? Rayanne wondered. Aileen was talking to Mrs Jefferson, who looked rather upset, glancing across the room towards her son. Rayanne sighed. Had Mrs Jefferson decided that Aileen would be the perfect wife and was she upset because things were not going the right way? she asked herself.

After dinner, following the others back to the drawing-room, Rayanne felt Cary's hand on her arm and he led her outside to the garden.

'Listen,' he said, 'the hyenas are out again.' She listened. The strange eerie howls made her shiver. They reminded her of that first terrifying night in the rondavel. Impulsively she turned to him.

'Did you put me in that awful rondavel in order to frighten me?' she asked abruptly. 'Were you trying to make me change my mind about staying?'

It was too dark to see his expression, but his fingers tightened round her arm. 'On the contrary, I was merely protecting you from the malicious gossip that might have ensued had I had you to stay here with no chaperone . . .' He sounded amused as he spoke. 'Can you imagine what Daphne and Christine would have said? I wonder if you have any idea just how malicious a frustrated female can be.'

Rayanne turned to him quickly. 'Why do you always say such nasty things about women? We're not all malicious. I think you're being absolutely hateful to poor Aileen, the way you ignore her. After all, she is your friend.'

'My friend?' He sounded amused. 'That's interesting. I met her once. How can you call her my friend? That reminds me—you never answered my question: why do you hate men so much? You always stiffen, look defiant, or on the defensive as if expecting an

100

attack. Surely you can't judge all men by your brothers' behaviour? No, I forgot.' His voice changed and became cold. 'You're not afraid of Burt West, that's obvious. What is it that Burt has that the rest of men lack? How come you're so relaxed with him, so at ease?'

'Am I?' Rayanne was startled. 'Yes, I am, I suppose,' she said thoughtfully.

'Why?' he asked again.

'I think because he treats me as an equal. He's never condescending, never corrects me, never patronising. He gives me the credit of having some brains.'

Cary groaned. 'Must we always have this, Ray? Who said you had no brains? I told you that you had. You've got a real chip on your shoulder about it, and you'll never be the real you until we've got rid of it.

'I doubt if that's possible. Twenty-two years of being made to feel inferior, of being laughed at and even despised . . .'

'Ray!' His hands caught her by the shoulders and he shook her. 'Stop it, do you hear me? No one considers you inferior, despicable, nor do they laugh at you.'

'They do!' Suddenly Rayanne felt desperate. 'Even your mother has stopped loving me. It was so wonderful when she fussed. I've never been treated like that before. She seemed to enjoy being with me, but she's changed. It's Aileen, now. Aileen, the perfect wife for her wonderful son,' Rayanne added bitterly.

His fingers dug into her flesh for a moment and then he released her, almost pushing her away.

'Just how stupid can you be!' he said angrily. 'Can't you see why Mother is doing that?'

'Doing what?'

'Oh, for crying out loud!' He gave a dramatic-sounding groan, took her arm and walked her down the lawn, into the utter darkness. In the distance the hyenas howled, an owl hooted and somewhere a lion growled. 'Look, Ray. Mother thinks she's being very clever. She forgets it's a method she's used as far back as I can remember. She has a theory that children, particularly sons, will always want what they can't have, so she believes that if she praises someone, I shall take an immediate dislike to that person. She has now decided that she's pushed you down my throat too much, having apparently forgotten this method and that by doing so she has made me have doubts about you. Now she dislikes Aileen very much. Why, I don't know. As I know, you think Aileen is a nice girl. She'll be a good wife to someone. That someone is not me. But Mother, bless her foolish little heart, thinks that if she now pushes Aileen at me, I shall revolt . . . Get it?' His fingers tightened round her arm. 'You do see what I mean?'

Rayanne drew a long deep breath. It didn't make sense . . . yet it did make sense, in a way. Just like everything else that happened in

102

this hot wonderful place, nothing really made sense, yet always did!

'I do see what you mean, but . . . but is it fair to Aileen?'

'Fair? I don't get it.'

'Well she loves you . . .'

Cary roared with laughter. 'Ray, sometimes you slay me,' he said, trying to control his mirth. 'Can anyone else be so naive, so . . .? Look, Aileen has been in and out of love with famous, wealthy men. She's always in the news. Why she's looked at me, I honestly don't know. But love . . . No, she doesn't love me.'

Rayanne hesitated. 'She . . . we talk quite a lot and . . . well . . .'

'Well?'

'Well I think she does.'

'You're wrong.' Cary turned round, leading her. 'We'd better go back or Mother will send a search party, fearing we've fallen into the crocs. No, Aileen doesn't love me at all. Not any more than you do. You've got quite a thing for Burt, haven't you?' he asked, his voice changing again.

'I like him.'

'Like? How does one define the difference between like and love?'

'There's a very big difference,' Rayanne said quickly.

'And what is it, if I may ask?' Cary was being his pompous self again. He must be angry about something, Rayanne thought.

'Liking . . . well, you enjoy being with the person because you're relaxed, you share interests, you make each other laugh.'

'That sounds to me more like an interpretation of love.'

'Oh, no,' she said earnestly. 'You can love someone and still feel uncomfortable when you're with him. When you love someone, you want to please him and you're often afraid of saying the wrong thing and hurting him. When you love someone you worry about that person being happy. You don't think of your own happiness, which is what you do when you *like* someone.'

'I see. I hadn't looked at it that way.' Cary led the way up the stairs to the *stoep*. 'Would you play for us tonight, Ray?' he asked. Mother and I did enjoy your music so much. Or are you nervous? I can't see why, when you play so well . . .'

Now she could see his face. He was staring at her in a strange way, a way she had never noticed before.

'You really want me to?' she asked.

'Yes, I do,' he told her.

'All right,' she said, 'I will.'

She went and sat by the spinet and lifted her hands, half closing her eyes. What should she think about?

Liking and loving . . . the difference between them. It was funny, because you could be so happy when you like someone, and so miserable when you love them.

Her fingers touched the keys, moving as if of their own accord. She liked Burt. How happy she was with him. But she loved Cary . . . she loved him so much, so very much, and yet there were times when life no longer had any reason, when she wondered why love had to be like that . . .

The sounds came wistful, puzzled, but with happy moments followed again by hesitation as if the pianist was trying to put her problems into the sound of music.

The others listened silently and when she had finished, clapped their praise.

'It's a shame you can't remember a tune,' Burt said. 'That would make a good record.'

CHAPTER FIVE

It was a strange situation, Rayanne thought. The days were full and the evenings pleasant. Sometimes she was happy, sometimes sad.

Cary might be right in saying his mother was trying to push poor Aileen at him, but Rayanne undoubtedly missed Mrs Jefferson's affection and fussiness. Now it was Aileen who apparently mattered; no longer Rayanne! Then there was Burt, still friendly, yet sometimes the way he spoke made Rayanne wonder if he was getting serious. This worried her, for their friendship would have to end if he wanted it to be more than just a pleasant friendship!

One afternoon, sitting quietly at the back of the lecture hall, looking at Cary as he stood on the dais, obviously at ease, joking as he told them about the time they had a baby elephant . . . she thought: 'How handsome he is in a rugged way.' A man of strength, determination. It didn't seem to make sense—this being chased by girls and letting his mother think she was matchmaking. Or was he right when he'd said she, Rayanne, had no idea of a real mother-and-child relationship?

She watched him tug at the lobe of his left ear as he described feeding the baby elephant with a bottle. Cary always tugged at his ear when he was searching for words. Not that he often had to seek, for he knew just what to say and when. How smooth his dark hair always looked; he never seemed to need a shave: this was something she liked in any man. That and good manners. These were important to her.

Yet suppose Cary did the impossible and loved her? Rayanne asked herself. Could she be happy living here? Could she? Unconsciously Rayanne shook her head. What a stupid question to ask herself. Of course she could!

Burt nudged her. 'What did he say? I didn't get it,' he whispered.

Rayanne stared, hardly seeing him, for her

thoughts were far away. 'What did he say? Well, I'm afraid I didn't hear either,' she admitted.

Burt shrugged and looked back at the dais. Rayanne looked, too. Now Cary was talking about baboons . . .

Was that why she came to these lectures? Not to learn or listen, but to look at Cary, relaxed, knowing no one was looking at her, not even Cary who might be watching with that amused supercilious smile she loathed. Did she loathe it? she asked herself. Of course she did!

After the lecture, Burt looked at her oddly. 'What were you dreaming about?' he asked.

They were caught up in the crowd of chattering, laughing students and swept along past the hostels to the big playing field where the students divided up to have some 'exercise'. Burt and Rayanne walked down the narrow hedge-lined lane that was a short cut to the house. Rayanne noticed that the hedge had been cut! So for once Cary had done what his mother wanted!

Later, lying in the deliciously refreshing bath water, Rayanne tried to think sensibly, even logically. What should she do? Finish her thesis, basing it on what she had learned here, and return to England?

She shivered. She could imagine her father's eyebrows going sky-high. 'You're soon back,' he'd say. 'Can't you settle down at anything?'

and then he'd sigh as if exasperated.

And her mother? She, too, would be disappointed. She had never said so in as many words, but Rayanne knew her mother would be relieved when her only daughter got married and was safely out of the way. With Rayanne at home, there were invariably scenes with her brothers. 'Why must you always quarrel with everyone?' her mother had once asked, in an exhausted voice.

'Because I won't let them get away with it,' Rayanne had said angrily. 'Just because I'm a girl . . .'

Her brothers? she asked herself. How they would laugh!

'Were you scared of the lions?' they'd ask, and probably pretend to bet that she'd run a mile the first time she saw a snake.

If only they would stop treating her like a . . . a nincompoop . . that was a good word for it. If only they would let her be a person, if they would respect her.

Respect. Maybe if she could find a way to make them *respect* her, they would stop their infuriating teasing. Well, wasn't that what she had come for? Six thousand miles in search of 'respect' and how far had she got? She hadn't even begun her thesis . . . all she had done was to fall crazily in love with a man who found women a *nuisance.*

She heard a hammering on her door and called out that she was in the bath. It was

Aileen's voice that replied.

'No hurry, Rayanne. I'll see you later. I've got some news.'

'Okay,' Rayanne called.

The warm refreshing bath had suddenly turned cold. She scrambled out, rubbing herself dry, choosing a soft lilac-coloured cotton frock. What good news could Aileen have? Rayanne wondered, as she peered anxiously in the mirror. Not that it really mattered what she looked like. She had long ago given up any attempt to equal Aileen's loveliness; or Christine's and Daphne's for that matter.

She went to the big picture window and looked out at the garden with its gradual slope to the river, the trees crowded close to the water with their bright flowers, and the distant mountains. It was so beaut . . .

She stopped seeing the view, as she saw Aileen and Cary, talking together. He was nodding, his face amused, and Aileen was talking excitedly, waving her hands about as she spoke. Was she telling him her 'good' news? Rayanne wondered. For although Aileen had only said the word *news,* her excited voice had added the word *good,* though it was not spoken.

Now Cary and Aileen were walking up the garden, Cary nodding his head as if in agreement. But it was Aileen who was so excited, putting her hand on his arm, pausing to stand in front of him as she talked.

Suddenly Rayanne was sure she knew what was going to happen next. The way Aileen looked up at him the way Cary smiled. In a moment, he would take her in his arms and kiss her.

Rayanne turned away quickly, hurrying to the door, going to the drawing room. Was Cary lying about Aileen? Were they really planning for their future? Had they allowed Mrs Jefferson to believe that she had organised the marriage, for that would give her a great deal of pleasure?

But if so, Cary had lied. Lied when he said he was not going to marry Aileen. Somehow it was hard to believe Cary to be a liar . . .

Burt was sitting opposite Mrs Jefferson. He looked up with a grin.

'Our hostess is trying to teach me to play chess. She's brilliant at it.'

Mrs Jefferson hardly glanced at Rayanne. 'I don't think Rayanne would enjoy it. It requires so much concentration,' she said, as she studied the little figures on the board. 'I'm not sure you're going to be good at it, either, Burt. Your mind wanders. Not like Aileen . . . She can concentrate and forget everything else,' Mrs Jefferson said proudly, almost as if Aileen was already her daughter.

Perhaps it was all settled, Rayanne thought, as she picked up a magazine lying on the long walnut coffee table and sat down. Perhaps it would be announced at dinner.

But it wasn't. Aileen and Cary came into the drawing room together and Cary handed out drinks. There was a general conversation over dinner which was, as usual, beautifully cooked and served. But Rayanne didn't enjoy it. She was waiting . . . and the longer she waited, the harder it got.

Aileen's eyes were shining and her voice kept rising excitedly even when she was talking about trivial matters. She kept looking at Cary and he would give her a little smile of understanding.

Perhaps it was that smile that hurt the most, for Rayanne, after dinner, pleaded a shocking migraine and an early night if they would excuse her.

Mrs Jefferson didn't even look up from the crochet she was doing. 'Of course. I hope you'll feel better in the morning.'

Cary was talking to Aileen, who was laughing, and neither looked up. Rayanne doubted if they had even heard what she had said. It was Burt who walked down the corridor with her, looking concerned.

'Is it very bad, Rayanne? Do you often get migraines? There's some very good drugs now for it. Is there anything you'd like?' he asked anxiously as he saw her to her bedroom door.

She shook her head. 'No, thanks, Burt. It's sweet of you, but all I really want is a dark room and sleep.'

The sleep was denied her, for she lay in bed, turning over, pummelling her pillows a dozen times. But she could not still her thoughts that seemed to be hurtling round her brain in circles.

Why was Aileen so excited, almost triumphant? Why was Cary suddenly devoting himself to Aileen, something he had never done before? Why did his mother look so complacent, so pleased with herself? It could only mean one thing . . . Yet did it? Round about twelve o'clock, there was a tap on Rayanne's door.

'Are you awake?' Aileen called gently, slightly opening the door.

Rayanne sat up, switched on the bedside light. 'Yes. Come in,' she said, her voice husky. Somehow she must act as if it meant nothing to her. Nothing at all.

Aileen came to sit on the edge of the bed. She was glowing with happiness.

'I just can't believe it's true,' she told Rayanne.

Rayanne tried to smile. 'What is true?'

'About Cary. I mean, for all his funny little ways, he really is terrific. Such a darling. I thought I'd have a hard battle, but it was amazingly easy. I just asked him and . . .'

'Asked him?' Rayanne almost gasped. Was it all right in these days of the so-called permissive society for the girl to make the proposal? she wondered.

112

Aileen nodded excitedly, her red hair swinging. 'Yes. You see there's this famous man, Alto Georgius. He's absolutely fabulous, right at the top, and knowing him would probably mean I'd get a job in South America at their research station, but it's terribly hard to get in. Someone told me Cary knew Alto quite well . . . that's why I came out here. It was sheer luck meeting his mother in Paris. Then I saw that in England he was talking at the conference, so I went along and introduced myself, and the rest . . .' she waved her hands about . . . 'easy as can be. I was frank with Cary, told him what I wanted, and he said he'd do what he could for me but would make no promise. Now he's been in touch with Alto and I'm to meet him in Cape Town. He's on tour round here and I may get the chance to go with him. Cary's coming, too, so it will be really great.'

Rayanne could only blink as she tried to grasp what she had been told. Aileen had come, not to 'hook'. Cary as Daphne would have described it, but in search of an important introduction. There had never been any question of Aileen being in love with him, she just wanted to *use* him.

Yet she obviously thought Cary wonderful . . . and if he went on this tour, too . . . Both such dedicated people, both sharing the same interests?

'I'm so glad for you,' Rayanne said, and

113

thought how weak it sounded. 'I really am.'

'I know,' Aileen smiled at her. 'It's been nice knowing you and having someone intelligent to talk to, at least. Maybe we'll meet again.'

'You're going?'

'Tomorrow. Burt's staying on, of course, because he and I are just friends. We have little in common.' Aileen stood up. 'This means so much to me, Rayanne. I just can't believe it's coming true!'

After Aileen had gone, Rayanne snuggled down in her bed. She felt dazed. She had wasted all that time feeling jealous of Aileen, envious, wondering when the wedding would be, when Aileen merely wanted something ...

But why couldn't Cary have told her? Rayanne asked herself. Why had he let her believe Aileen was chasing him? Was it a sign that he knew Rayanne was in love with him and it amused him to see her hurt and anxious? No, surely not, she told herself. Cary wasn't cruel. He couldn't be deliberately cruel, of that she was sure.

However, next day after Aileen had said farewell and Mike Crisp driven her to the airport, Rayanne wondered if Cary could be deliberately cruel, after all. Burt had vanished, saying he wanted to develop some films. Mrs Jefferson was busy talking to the gardeners about their work for the day. So Rayanne found herself temporarily alone with Cary in the garden, drinking ice-cold drinks under the

114

trees.

'Well?' Cary asked, his voice amused. 'She wasn't after me, after all, as you thought. At least, not in the same sense!'

Inside Rayanne, anger stirred slightly. 'You gave me the impression that she was.'

He laughed. 'What a joke! If I really thought every girl was after me, I'd end up an egoist.'

'You're one now, I think.'

'I thought you probably did. A proper monster, that's how you see me, isn't it?' He laughed again. 'Well, at least Aileen knows where she's heading. Ambitious, hardworking, determined to succeed—what a horrible mixture for a woman!'

Rayanne sat up stiffly. 'And why shouldn't she be ambitious, hardworking and determined to succeed? Can you give me any reason why that makes her a horrible mixture? Aileen is not only most attractive but a very nice person!' She paused, for she saw he was trying not to laugh, his eyes amused. 'So . . .' she began, and stopped.

'So what? Maybe I'm an exception, but I like my women feminine and helpless,' Cary said. 'A successful woman is usually a pathetic creature.'

'And why should she be pathetic and a man not?' Rayanne asked, indignantly again.

Cary chuckled. 'I didn't say that a man wasn't. You're quoting my words before

115

they're spoken.'

'The way you spoke implied that you meant women only.'

'Well,' Cary spoke thoughtfully, 'let's face it, Ray. Women mean well but usually fail by trying too hard to succeed.'

A cold finger seemed to slide down her back. 'Now that's a nasty thing to say!'

He looked astonished, even perhaps a little hurt.

'It wasn't meant to be.' He spoke almost accusingly. 'Now you're looking at my words out of context. What I meant was that because women are idealists, they often tackle more than they can finish.'

'Isn't that better than tackling nothing?'

Cary tugged thoughtfully at the lobe of his left ear.

'You could be right . . .' Rayanne felt a warm flush of triumph, for he had admitted it. 'I suppose,' he added, spoiling it with his scepticism.

'Do you succeed in doing everything you tackle?' she demanded.

He smiled. 'Of course not.'

'Then why . . .' she began, then stopped. Sighing, she looked at him. What was the good of arguing? They could talk all night and get nowhere. He was too clever. You could never hope to win and he knew it, and let you know he knew it, too.

She was surprised when he suddenly leant

forward and took hold of her hand 'Don't look so stricken, little Ray. I think women are wonderful.'

Jerking her hand free, she glared at him. 'You don't, you know you don't. You like to make fun of us, make us look fools. That's what you like doing. You men are all the same, you make use of us, but you don't respect us or . . . or . . .' She had to stop, for her voice was frighteningly unsteady.

He moved with a swiftness that startled her, kneeling in front of her, his hands on the arms of her chair so that she could not escape.

'We do love you,' he said, supplying the word she had been unable to say. 'Otherwise we wouldn't marry you. What you women don't seem to understand is that the average man suffers from an inferiority complex. We're fully aware that you women are not only highly intelligent, but much stronger than we are, and we're so terrified that you're going to dominate us, we have to try to make you feel small and insignificant. Can you really blame us? It's a battle for survival.'

His face was frighteningly close to hers. For once, she could see herself in his eyes. She felt herself trembling and his eyes began to twinkle. As usual, he was teasing her.

This arrogant, hateful . . . she began to think, but her thoughts slid to a standstill. Arrogant, perhaps, but hateful, no, quite definitely no.

'Ray,' he said. 'Oh, Ray, why do you rise to the bait so quickly?'

And suddenly she was laughing.

'You are the end,' she told him. 'The positive end!'

He chuckled. 'Play it cool, baby,' he joked. 'This is just a beginning.'

He leaned forward and lightly kissed her cheek.

'See you,' he said, rising to his feet with incredible speed, and she found herself alone, sitting back, still shaking a little, and watched him go with his long rapid strides towards the house.

What had he meant? she wondered. *Just a beginning...?*

*   *   *

Slowly Rayanne followed Cary into the house, meeting his mother when she reached it.

'Dear child,' Mrs Jefferson said warmly as she took Rayanne's hands in hers. 'I'm so glad that girl has gone. She was such a bore.'

Rayanne stared. 'I thought you liked her.'

'Liked her?' Mrs Jefferson laughed. 'I couldn't bear her, but she was Cary's friend, after all, and I had to be polite. I'm glad we're on our own again.'

Later Burt said much the same. 'I can't stand that type of career woman. She can talk of nothing but her work. Anyone would think

118

my work was utterly unimportant.'

'I thought you were a friend of hers,' Rayanne said.

He laughed. 'So we are, but even friends know the truth about one another. She uses me. I can be useful at times because I know the right people. Apart from that, she has no time for me. I bore her.'

'But, Burt, you've never bored me,' Rayanne said impulsively, then regretted it, for she saw the light in his eyes as he turned to her.

'I don't?'

They were walking along the lawn, just above the edge of the river. Several crocodiles were asleep on the hot sand and Burt was taking photographs of them. He had a film camera and wanted the crocs to move, but stubbornly they refused, their eyes tightly closed.

'Well, we seem able to talk about anything,' said Rayanne. 'We argue about everything, and it's fun.'

He laughed. 'That's the difference between you and Aileen. In Aileen's eyes, only one person can possibly be right—Aileen Hampton. *You're* always ready to admit that the other fellow could be right. Then one can argue. Oh, Aileen's not bad, actually I'm quite fond of her, but she does rather send me round the bend with her know-all. These dedicated women drive me mad!'

'Cary said much the same,' Rayanne told him, pausing to toss a pebble into the still water that hardly rippled in response.

'He did?' Burt laughed. 'He made it pretty plain that he had no time for her. She only wanted that introduction, you know. You thought she was after him—Cary, I mean, didn't you?' He laughed again. 'You and those two birds, Daphne and Christine. What do you see in Cary that makes him so special?'

Rayanne caught her breath. Had Burt discovered the truth? She breathed again as he went on casually:

'I can see that most girls would find him attractive, that rather arrogant superman sort of behaviour of his has a strange charm. But he's so dedicated to his work. I doubt if he'll ever marry.'

'I doubt it, too,' Rayanne said, unaware of just how wistful her voice was; nor did she see the quick look Burt gave her and the cloud that seemed to come over his face.

'Whoever he does marry will have a tough life,' he said, his voice almost sulky.

'Yes, I guess so.' Rayanne sighed. 'But it would be worth it.' Even as she spoke, she realised what she had said. Feeling her cheeks growing hot, she managed a laugh, and added: ' If she really loves him.'

Burt put away his camera. 'Hopeless waiting here,' he said curtly. 'Let's go back. We'll try another day.'

Walking over the lawn, he looked at her. 'What is this thing called love?' he asked.

'I sometimes wonder,' sighed Rayanne, walking slowly, her eyes watchful as she stared at the house, wondering where Cary was. 'It seems to me you can be very happy with someone and like him very much and yet not love him, while you can love someone and be unhappy with him because . . .' She paused.

Burt looked at her. 'Because?'

'Because he doesn't love you.' She laughed. '*C'est la vie,* as Harold would say. He's my eldest brother and he's always being philosophical. It drives you mad. No matter how bad things are he always grins and says *c'est la vie.* Suppose it is *life,* but that's no comfort.'

'You've got five brothers?' Burt asked. 'I'm an only child.'

'I wish I was,' Rayanne said quickly.

Burt shook his head. 'You wouldn't if you were. It's lonely. Besides, they expect too much of you when you're the only one.'

'They do when they're five of them. Imagine my life—with a father and five brothers all waiting for me to do something dramatically important, important enough for them to say proudly: "My sister is a . . ." or better still, "Just think what my daughter has done!" That's what they're waiting for, and what on earth can I do to satisfy them?'

Burt looked at her. 'This is the chip on your

shoulder, is it?' he asked.

Startled, she turned. 'Has Cary been talking to you about me?'

'Sure. Why not? We've both noticed your moods.'

'I do not have moods,' she said indignantly.

'Oh no?' Burt laughed. 'I'd say you have more silent moods than any girl I know. An aura of anger surrounds you and sometimes the way you glare at poor Cary makes me wonder he doesn't go up in smoke.'

'I do not glare at Cary!'

'Oh no? Maybe I should have a candid camera around some time. Might shock you, rather. Why do you hate him so?'

'I do not hate him!' she said angrily.

'Don't you? Yet you get mad at the slightest thing he says.'

'It's because he will tease me, and I hate . . .'

'Being teased?' Burt laughed. 'Yet you let me tease you.'

'Well . . .' Rayanne hesitated. 'You tease differently.'

'Is that a compliment or the reverse?'

It was a question Rayanne couldn't answer; or, at least, she couldn't tell *him*, though she knew the answer all right. It didn't matter when Burt teased her because it didn't matter to her *what* he thought!

'A compliment, of course,' she said, uncomfortably aware of a keen look in his eyes as he stared at her. Whatever happened, he mustn't know the truth. Suppose he told Cary . . .?

'Actually, according to Cary,' Burt went on, so Rayanne began to walk again, wishing she could end the conversation, 'you hate all men. I didn't think you hated me.'

'Of course I don't hate you, and I certainly don't hate *all* men. Only just a few.'

'And Cary is one of them?'

'Oh, look!' Rayanne turned to him again angrily. 'Leave me alone. How do I know if I hate him or not? What is hate, anyhow? I admire him very much, I like him . . . sometimes. He maddens me, makes me angry and then laughs at me. Naturally that makes me furious, yet he has a gift of making me laugh with him Not *at* him, but with him. against myself. No, I don't think I could say I hate him, but . . .'

'Rayanne, dear child, I'm going shopping tomorrow. I wondered if you'd like to come with me?' Mrs Jefferson, coming carefully down the few steps from the *stoep* to meet them, called.

'I'd love to,' answered Rayanne. 'I haven't seen any of the countryside yet.'

'There isn't much to see—except bushes and trees and mountains,' Burt told her.

'Now, Burt,' Mrs Jefferson said with a smile, 'that's not really fair. There's a lot of beauty round here.'

123

Rayanne agreed next day when they left the house. Rather to her mixed dismay and pleasure, she found herself sitting next to Cary. Mrs Jefferson had insisted on sitting in the back. It was more comfortable, she said, but Rayanne, glancing at Cary, saw the smile playing round his mouth and knew that Mrs Jefferson had made it up; that normally she preferred the front, but she wanted to put Cary and Rayanne together! Oh, these matchmaking mothers, Rayanne thought. If only they would leave you alone!

The day was intensely hot. Her dress was wet before she even left the house. There wasn't the slightest wind and she wondered how the old lady could bear it. But Mrs Jefferson seemed content and looking forward to her shopping.

'Luckily Cary has business to do, so we can enjoy ourselves, Rayanne,' Mrs Jefferson said, propped up in the corner of the car with various cushions Cary had found for her. 'Some of the shops are quite good.'

The earth road continued a long way, running alongside the high wire fence. They saw few wild animals, only a dozen giraffes galloping off with their funny movements away from the sound of the car.

At last the car was on the main road. This was also earth, but much more level, so the

124

violent jerks and shakes that had been their lot up to then, no longer happened.

Perlee was a small town, but as Mrs Jefferson had said, there were several very good dress shops with the latest fashions. Mrs Jefferson needed some new clothes, she said, would Rayanne help her decide what to wear?

'I like crazy clothes, but Cary, dear boy, is very conservative about what his mother should wear. However,' she laughed, 'I lay no store by what he says. I do what I like, and I tell him so. Don't you think I'm right?'

'Absolutely,' Rayanne agreed. She sat on a chair in the little fitting room while Mrs Jefferson struggled to get into a pale orange trouser suit.

'What do you think?' Mrs Jefferson twisted and turned to try to see her back view in the mirror.

'It does something to you,' said Rayanne, and it did. Besides, why shouldn't Cary's mother wear what she liked? After all, when you get old, Rayanne thought, there can be very few pleasures to enjoy, so why not let her enjoy this?

'Good!' Mrs Jefferson beamed. 'What about you?' She turned to the assistant. 'Have you any really thin clothes? My young friend feels the heat very much.'

Rayanne hesitated. Did she really need any more *thin* clothes? After all, she couldn't stay

125

there for ever, and they'd be far too thin to wear in an English summer.

The assistant brought two dresses, one leaf-green and one snow-white.

'They look just you, Rayanne my dear,' Mrs Jefferson said eagerly. 'Do try them on.'

So Rayanne did, and Mrs Jefferson was right. They were perfect—light, beautifully thin and comfortable. But were they really necessary?

'Do have them, Rayanne,' a deep voice said.

Rayanne swung round, startled. Cary stood in the doorway, smiling at them. She was wearing the leaf-green dress.

'You like it?' she asked.

He shrugged. 'Does that matter? The important thing is that *you* like them, so why not have them?'

'Why not, indeed?' his mother chimed in. It's going to get hotter in the days ahead, Rayanne, dear child. You're going to need them.'

Rayanne stared at Cary. Should she ask him how long she could stay? His eyes met hers and there was a moment of silence. Rayanne had the strangest of feelings—that he could read her thoughts.

'Yes, Ray,' he said gravely, 'take them. You're going to need them.'

126

CHAPTER SIX

That evening was strange, Rayanne thought, but they all seemed to miss Aileen. Dinner was a quiet meal despite the excellently-cooked food Mrs Jefferson's cook, Matilda, had prepared for them. There were sudden silences that seemed to last for ever.

Afterwards as they drank coffee in the drawing-room, Mrs Jefferson sighed.

'I think I'll go to bed,' she told them.'I have what feels like a migraine on its way.'

Rayanne walked with the old lady. 'You'll be all right?' she asked anxiously.

Mrs Jefferson smiled. 'Quite all right. It's been a trying time for us all,' she said, and closed the door.

Puzzled, Rayanne stood for a moment in the corridor. She could hear the cicadas humming away and an occasional howl of some wild animal coming from the distance. What had Mrs Jefferson meant? she wondered. 'It's been a trying time for us all.' Mrs Jefferson seemed to be rather confused; one moment she was saying she found Aileen both boring and tiring, the next she obviously missed her. One moment she had almost ignored Rayanne, making a fuss of Aileen, the next being glad Aileen had gone, and fussing over Rayanne! And now?

Back in the drawing room, the two men were silent as Rayanne joined them. She poured them all a second cup of coffee and the silence remained. Suddenly she laughed:

'You know, it's odd, but we all miss Aileen.'

Cary looked up, his face creased with a frown. 'And why should it be odd?' he asked. 'Aileen is intelligent and interesting to talk to Very dedicated to her work.'

Rayanne felt the colour in her cheeks. 'Oh, I wasn't suggesting that she wasn't interesting. We used to talk for hours in my room at night. It's just that . . . well, I understand she hopes to go on this lecture tour with . . . I can't remember his name.'

Cary stared at her, his face grave. 'Yes, Alto Georgius. I hope to join her. It should not only be an interesting tour but may really help us make people see how important conservation is.'

'You're joining her?' Burt sounded surprised.

'Yes, I am,' Cary said quietly.

Burt whistled softly. 'Look, Christine's giving a party to the visiting staff. She asked me, but I thought I'd be playing chess with your ma, Cary, so I said No, but there's nothing much to do, so let's go.' He smiled at Rayanne. 'Coming?'

She hesitated. 'I wasn't asked.' She and Christine had hardly exchanged more than a dozen words, and those only when Christine

128

had no choice, for Cary was there.

Surprisingly Cary laughed. 'Neither was I. Somehow I don't think they're the sort of parties Ray enjoys, Burt.'

Burt looked annoyed. 'Well, we must do something. We can't just sit here.' He looked at Rayanne. 'Let's go and see Samantha and Mike. I met him earlier today and he said something about fixing it for me to go and film that new baboon family 'You can talk to Samantha, she'll be glad to see us. She's pretty fed-up, and I can't say I blame her. It's like being married to a football fan. Mike thinks of nothing but his work. Tough on the wife.'

'No more tough than being married to a doctor, a merchant seaman . . . or practically any marriage, for a wife has to accept her husband's involvement with his work,' Cary said quietly—a quietness that made Rayanne shiver for a moment. She knew he was angry about something. But what was it? she wondered. She was even more frightened when he suddenly turned to her and snapped: 'How often do you see Samantha?'

She blinked for a moment. 'Not as often as I should, I suppose,' she told him. 'We do sometimes pop in for coffee, don't we, Burt? Also if Burt isn't with me, I get Kwido to take me there on my way back.'

'I see.' Cary's dark tufty eyebrows seemed about to meet as he frowned. 'You say you don't see her as often as you should. I wonder if you're not seeing her too much.'

'Too much?' Rayanne's voice rose with surprise.

Cary nodded. 'Yes, too much.' His voice was cold. 'Sister Macintyre has been talking to me about Samantha. She says that Samantha's condition has gradually grown worse since you came here.'

'Condition?'

He nodded. 'Daphne Macintyre reckons she's on the verge of a nervous breakdown— Samantha is, I mean.' He frowned again. 'She's got steadily more depressed, resentful and full of ailments that don't really exist. Daphne reckons that Samantha is like a child, trying to gain attention.'

'She needs it,' said Burt, almost growling. Cary glanced at him, but ignored the remark as he went on:

'As I told you when you first came, Ray, I'm not happy about the wardens' wives meeting girls like you. It makes them discontented, resenting their isolation. After all, surely a wife's duty is to share her husband's interests. I seem to remember you telling me that once.'

Rayanne caught her breath as her cheeks grew hot. She could remember it, too, so plainly. Also the soft gentle way he had answered her, saying: 'I think that's rather wonderful.'

'Mike's a good chap. I'd hate to see his marriage threatened,' Cary finished.

It was Burt now who was angry, so angry that his voice trembled. 'Look, Cary, if you want to see someone who is threatening the Crisps' marriage, it's that Daphne Macintyre. She hasn't an ounce of brains in her head nor a soft spot in that hard heart of hers. Every time Samantha goes to the Clinic, Daphne starts talking about the essential ingredients of a contented marriage, which is to share interests and have children . . .'

'And what's wrong with that?' Cary snapped.

Burt scowled. 'Daphne hasn't a clue what marriage requires. Children are not essential—they may even harm a marriage. In this case, though, I think it's the answer, but it isn't exactly tactful of Daphne to harp on it when Samantha and Mike have been trying to have a child for the last five years. It's like twisting a knife in a wound. Samantha always comes back in tears.'

'You seem to know a lot about Samantha,' Cary said gruffly.

Burt smiled. 'Sure I do. Mike and I are real buddies, but Samantha weeps on my shoulder.' Then he frowned. 'Look, let's get this straight. If Samantha has got worse since Rayanne came, it's not her fault—Rayanne's, I mean. It's Daphne's. As for Rayanne, if anything, she's tried to interest Samantha in her husband's work. All Rayanne talks about these days is the importance of conservation.'

He smiled across the room at Rayanne who was sitting very still, her hands tightly clutched together. 'She's getting even worse than you, Cary, and never stops talking about it.'

'Daphne Macintyre has been in charge of the Clinic for several years,' Cary said, in the rather pompous way he sometimes used and which Rayanne hated. 'I have no record of Daphne making a wrong diagnosis. She's seriously concerned for Samantha and that a nervous breakdown might occur.'

Rayanne found her voice.'That's absolute rubbish, Cary! Samantha isn't like that. She's just bored and lonely. Mike is out all day and most nights he's studying or making notes. He has a lot of paperwork, as you know.' She sighed. 'Burt is right, you know, Cary. The Crisps want a baby—so badly. If only . . .'

Burt suddenly clapped his hands. 'I've got it! What fools we were not to think about it before.'

He smiled as he turned to Rayanne. 'Look, if they can't have one, they could adopt one. Lots of people adopt children and then have some of their own. They say it's because the mother stops worrying about it, and . . .'

Cary stood up. His face might have been carved out of stone, it was so cold and lifeless.

'I would prefer you to refrain from interfering with the private lives of my employees, Burt. It's their affair, not yours. There are some people who find it impossible to accept other men's children. It's possible Mike feels that way.'

'Then Mike would be plain selfish,' Rayanne said indignantly.

Cary looked at her. 'Would he? Or would it be Samantha who was being selfish?' He glanced at his watch. 'I've some letters to write, so if you'll excuse me . . .' He left hurriedly.

Burt whistled softly as he looked across the room. 'He's really mad tonight. I wonder what's rattled him. I didn't think he was that partial to Aileen Hampton's charm, but seems like he's missing her.' He stood up. 'Come along, Rayanne, let's go and see the Crisps. I can take the Land Rover I usually have.'

He pulled Rayanne to her feet and went on holding her hands, smiling down at her, swinging her hands gently.

'Or shall we stay here, alone?' he asked, his eyes twinkling. 'A romantic setting. I could put on some music, turn low the lights . . .'

Of course he was joking, Rayanne told herself, but a shiver went down her back. Was he? Sometimes there was a look in his eyes that frightened her. Not that she was *afraid* of Burt—but she liked him too much to want to hurt him. Perhaps it was just her imagination, but . . .

She managed a laugh. 'Let's go and see Samantha and Mike, Burt. I wonder if they've ever discussed adopting a child. It might really be the answer.'

They went outside into the perfumed dark night with the sky's blackness broken by the beauty of the new moon. Rayanne looked up.

'It's unbelievable that man has been up there . . .'

Burt's hand was under her elbow as he guided her across the drive to the Land Rover. 'Many things are unbelievable today.' He paused and for one moment Rayanne thought he was going to take her in his arms. What should she do? she wondered wildly. He was too nice to hurt. She couldn't slap his face, or turn hers away . . . nor could she let him kiss her and believe that she loved him.

At that moment, a light flooded out from the house and a door of the *stoep* opened. Cary's voice carried clearly through the quiet air.

'Ask Mike to ring me first thing in the morning and I'll give him the answer he needs,' Cary called.

'Okay, Boss!' Burt called back, and helped Rayanne into the Rover. Sitting by her side, switching on the ignition, he chuckled. 'I wonder how long he'd been watching us.'

'Watching us?' Rayanne was startled. 'Why should he watch us?'

'Because he's that kind of guy,' Burt said, the engine roaring into life. 'He sees us all as his puppets and he dislikes us playing unless he's pulling the strings.'

'I don't think that's quite fair!'

134

'Fair it may not be, but it's true. Cary knew from the first time he met Aileen in London just what she wanted of him, but he had a good inner laugh at the way he made her behave. Rushing out here suddenly so that he couldn't get out of it, being so biddable, which Cary adores. He loves to crack the whip and watch his women obey.'

'His women?' Rayanne echoed.

'Yes, aren't you all smitten by his charm? If you're not, you ought to be. Leastways, that's how Cary sees it. He just laps it all up. I doubt if Christine and Daphne would have been here so long if they didn't make out they were fighting to hook him.' Burt gave a funny laugh. 'Now he's trying to catch you. Then he'll make you dance, regardless of whether you'll get hurt or not.'

'I don't believe it!' Rayanne turned in her seat to stare at Burt angrily. 'It's not true.'

Burt chuckled. 'Isn't it? You only say that because you don't want to believe it. You hate believing things that are nasty, don't you? You like life to be smooth and perfect, everyone an angel. Unfortunately none of us are angels—that's why you're so hurt when you learn the truth about us. You see life through rose-coloured glasses . . . at least you'd like to, and when people behave normally, you get upset. Take your reaction just now. You were shocked, horrified and hurt because I dared say anything against the one and only Cary

135

Jefferson. He has to be perfect. Just as I have to be perfect, too.'

'You?' Rayanne was really startled.

His hand closed over hers for a moment. 'Yes, and you know darned well why. You hate being disillusioned, because it breaks down something inside you. You have such high expectations. We've all got to be as perfect as your father.'

'My father?' Rayanne began to laugh, but stopped. 'My father?' she repeated.

'Yes, you've got a real complex there. You're always talking about your wretched brothers who seem to spend their life deliberately hurting you by teasing. The plain truth is this: you hate them teasing you because it makes you look small in front of your father. You want your father's love. You need it.' The Rover had stopped and they were parked outside the Crisps' house.

'You need it very much,' Burt went on, his voice low and earnest. 'You want his respect, his praise and for him to be proud of you. You'll never be the real you until that happens.' He leant across and opened the Rover's door. 'We'd better go in or Samantha will think we're necking.' He chuckled. 'What a hope!'

Silently Rayanne followed him up the few steps to the door. Samantha flung it open and called out in delight.

'Come in, come in. The answer to a lonely

girl's prayer! Lovely to see you, Burt . . . and you, too Rayanne Why this unexpected visit?'

'The evening was dead,' Burt said bluntly. 'Looks like we all miss Miss Hampton.' His voice was sarcastic. 'Mrs J. has retired with a sprouting migraine, Cary has gone to write some letters and we . . . well, we thought we'd like to see you.'

'You know I'm delighted. I'll make us some coffee. Dorcas has gone home, of course. Come in the kitchen with me, Rayanne. Mike's in his office, Burt.'

Samantha, in a long lush-looking housecoat of peacock colours, led the way to the kitchen, talking over her shoulder.

'It's so nice to see you, Rayanne.' Then she smiled and lifted her hand, wagging one finger warningly. 'Watch out, though. You were a long time sitting out there with Burt.' She laughed. 'Don't look so shocked. Why don't you marry him? He's crazy about you.'

Crazy about me, Rayanne thought. Was he really? But she . . . was crazy about someone else.

CHAPTER SEVEN

In the morning at breakfast, Cary seemed to have become his usual self. He greeted Rayanne cheerfully, looked at Burt and asked

137

them:

'We're catching some hippos today to send to England. Like to come along?'

'I would,' Rayanne said eagerly.

'Is it kind to take animals who are used to the lovely African sunshine to cold England?' Mrs Jefferson asked, carefully eating her grapefruit.

Cary shrugged. 'They soon seem to adjust in a land where the sun never shines.'

'It does shine,' Rayanne said quickly. 'Sometimes we have beautifully hot summers.'

'Sometimes?' Cary looked at her, a smile playing round his mouth and her cheeks went bright red.

Once again, she had risen to the bait!

'I think most foreigners are surprised just how often the English sun does shine,' Burt joined in quickly. 'Most of them think it always rains.'

'It can be very cold in Africa,' Mrs Jefferson agreed. 'In Johannesburg, now . . .' she shivered, 'it can be very cold indeed.'

'How do you manage—I mean, it can't be easy to get a huge hippo into a crate,' said Rayanne, wanting to change the conversation.

'We keep them in paddocks for some time,' Cary explained. 'Their food is put in the travelling box so they get used to walking into it and there's no difficulty. It's been done so often these days that there are no real problems.'

138

'I think you're very clever, dear,' Mrs Jefferson said, helping herself from the sideboard where the deliciously cooked kidneys and bacon were.

'It's not me, Mother. I just organise things and leave the rest to the staff. Nowadays we use a new anaesthetic that's very successful. It's a synthetic-morphinous one and it affects the brain and central nervous system. It's much more powerful than morphia and releases the animal from its inhibitions. This means that an animal is subdued. There is also a sleeping draught mixed with it, so the animal moves like a sleepwalker.'

'You've gone a long way,' Burt commented, 'from the old days when you caught them with lassos.'

Cary laughed. 'We certainly have! Those were the days—the battles we had! You should try to handle a giraffe with his long legs. This is infinitely easier and kinder to the animals as they rarely get hurt.'

'But how do you give them the injection?' Mrs Jefferson asked. 'A bow and arrow, I suppose.'

'We use a crossbow and dart now. We used also to use a gas gun, but the crossbow goes off quietly so the animals aren't frightened. Also the dart can be shot accurately a very long way. It can be a hundred and twenty yards, though the dart can be affected by the wind changes, so it's better to use it in the wooded regions, otherwise the wind makes it difficult.'

'Does it hurt the poor creature?'

Cary smiled patiently at his mother. 'I doubt it, because it happens so swiftly. The dart looks like an ordinary hypodermic syringe with a tail added. After we've finished with the animal, he's given an antidote and speedily regains his usual senses. Meanwhile all that has happened is a small wound which we will have treated with disinfectant. Nothing to worry about.'

'So long as you're not catching elephants, Cary.'

'Actually they're not difficult. Once they're sleepy they move so slowly and seem to behave as we want them to. The difficulty, of course, is in choosing which animals we want to catch. We have Bilkington who does most of the shooting. He's a fine biologist. You've probably heard of him, Ray?' Cary turned to her.

She shook her head. 'Afraid I haven't.'

'How long does it take for the drug to work?' Burt asked.

'About ten minutes. Gradually their running slows down and finally we catch up with them. Bit rough, for they charge through bushes and trees. Ray won't be allowed to leave the Rover,' Cary added with a smile.

'Why . . .' Rayanne began to ask, but Mrs Jefferson got in first.

'I should hope not indeed! Now, Cary, you're to take great care of Rayanne. What

140

would her Uncle Joe say if anything happened to her? How could I write and tell him? He'd never forgive me . . .' Mrs Jefferson began to sound quite hysterical.

'I won't let her run any risks, Mother,' Cary said gravely. 'My main problem is the fact that she resents being protected and is quite capable of jumping out of the Rover and being eaten by a lion—out of sheer defiance.' He smiled at Rayanne.

'Rayanne, you wouldn't?' Mrs Jefferson was shocked.

Rayanne blushed. He was so right! 'I won't, Mrs Jefferson.'

'You promise? Please, Rayanne, I shan't be able to stand it unless you promise you won't do anything foolish and that you'll . . . well, do what Cary says. He does know, you know?'

'I promise,' Rayanne said with a smile. 'Please don't worry about me. I know I'm in good hands.'

'We all know that,' Cary said dryly. His voice had changed again. 'By the way, how is the thesis coming along, Ray?' he asked.

She was so startled that for a moment she couldn't answer. Now why had he suddenly asked her that? And what could she tell him? Not even the first page had been written yet, nor did it seem likely that it would ever be. There was a strange silence and she suddenly became aware that three pairs of eyes were staring at her, that three people were waiting

141

expectantly for her answer.

It was a great effort, but she managed a somewhat uncertain laugh. 'Not too badly, thanks. Copious notes, of course, but I'm still not quite sure from which angle . . .'

Cary stood up, rattling his chair on the highly polished floor.

'Today may give you inspiration. See you in half an hour. Burt, you bring her along and we'll all meet at Jock Tilling's house. See you,' he added curtly, and left the room.

Rayanne buttered her piece of toast slowly, grateful that Burt was talking to Mrs Jefferson. What had Cary meant? she wondered. Was it a gentle hint that he thought it time she left the Jefferson Wild Life Reserve?

'Is it very hard to write a thesis, Rayanne, dear child?' Mrs Jefferson asked anxiously.

'Well, not really . . .' Rayanne began, and saw the look in Burt's eyes. He didn't believe she was writing one, she realised. He thought it was all an excuse . . . just as Christine and Daphne had done. 'The trouble is . . .' she went on, but Burt interrupted.

'To know what you're writing about,' Burt said dryly, 'and why. However, I imagine she'll have to do it.'

'Why are you so sure?' Mrs Jefferson asked. 'I mean, is it so important? Couldn't she change her mind?'

Burt looked across the table at Rayanne 'I very much doubt it. What do you say,

142

Rayanne?' he asked, looking at her. It was a strange feeling, she thought. It was almost mesmeric, the way his eyes held hers so that she couldn't look away. Then he smiled, moving his head, releasing her from that strange moment. 'No, she'll write that thesis all right, make no mistake.'

Rayanne got up quickly. 'If you'll excuse me, Mrs Jefferson, I think I'd better change into my working gear.'

She saw the amusement in Burt's eyes. He knew she was running away, unable to answer the question. He was right and yet he was wrong. She had not come here because she wanted to meet Cary, that was for sure. She had honestly come in the hope that she would find out what she really wanted to do . . . but was that the truth? she asked herself as she hurried to her room. She had come out to, as Burt had said, prove herself. Prove that she could do something to make her father proud of her; prove that she wasn't a moron!

It didn't take her long to change into the khaki trews and thin matching shirt she had recently bought in the town, that was not really so far away, once you had accepted Africa's standards where you thought nothing of driving ninety miles to meet someone. Then she went out on to the screened *stoep*.

She stood very still, looking at the beautiful view before her. The distant mountains, now a strange greyish green as the sun shone on them. The trees were so straight, reminding her of soldiers on parade. How beautiful it all was, she thought. How could she bear to leave it? To go back to city life, to the noise and the mad rushing of cars which seemed determined to be lethal in their behaviour. Here it was so peaceful, so lovely. Just look at the fascinating colours! Lines of freshly-red land where it had been ploughed. And closer to the house, the slow reluctantly-moving river. Odd, but she never thought of crocodiles these days. Somehow she had unconsciously adapted herself to this new life.

A tiny lizard scuttled across the floor and up the wall. She watched it, fascinated by its movements. How wonderful to be able to run up a straight wall like that! She looked back at the garden with the great bushes, heavily laden with bright red and yellow flowers while the little birds with their long curving beaks, hovered over them, seeking for pollen, moving like miniature helicopters. It was all so lovely . . . how could she bear to leave it?

Her eyes stung warningly and she pressed her hand against her mouth as she fought the tears she mustn't shed. She would have to go, she knew that. Beyond shadow of doubt, she would have to go eventually. Eventually? And what did that mean? Was Cary's question about her thesis a gentle hint that he wanted her to go?

But how could she go?

And the thesis? Did Cary believe it was all made up as Burt so obviously did, and Christine and Daphne, too?

The thesis must be written. It had to be written, Rayanne told herself sternly. It was time she pulled herself together. That very night she would do a skeleton draft of what it was to be about. Maybe Cary was right and the day ahead of them would help her know *what* to concentrate on. There was so much . . .

Someone banged on the door and Burt shouted: Aren't you ready yet? We don't want our heads chopped off because we're late.'

'I'm coming,' Rayanne called. 'Coming right now!' Hastily she grabbed her powder compact and studied her eyes anxiously. No, thanks be, there was no evidence of the tears she had so nearly shed.

She hurried out to join him and Mrs Jefferson was hovering.

'You did promise, Rayanne,' she said anxiously. 'You will be careful?'

Impulsively Rayanne kissed her. 'Of course I will,' she promised. How lovely it was to have someone who cared, she thought.

Bumping along the earth road in the Land Rover, she glanced at Burt. 'I do wish I could drive.'

He smiled. 'I'll teach you.'

'You would?' she said eagerly.

'Why not? We'll get out of the Reserve as we can't risk stalling the engine if a huge angry

145

elephant came chasing us.' He chuckled. 'You want to learn?'

'Oh, so badly!' Her voice was earnest. 'I couldn't learn from everyone.'

'You feel you could learn from me?' He glanced at her and she looked back at his kind face, his thoughtful eyes.

'Yes,' she told him, 'I could. You'd be patient and understanding.'

'What about Cary?' Burt's voice was suddenly harsh. 'Could you learn from him?'

Rayanne hesitated, twisting her fingers together, glancing at them to avoid looking at the man by her side.

'I don't know,' she said slowly. 'I never feel quite at ease with Cary. He changes his mood so suddenly. One moment I'm relaxed and we're getting on well, the next moment he's quite different—pompous, even cold.' She gave a little laugh. 'How disloyal of me when he's been so kind and generous. All the same . . .' she gave Burt a quick smile and then wished she hadn't, for she saw the hope in his eyes, 'I'd rather learn from you.'

'Good enough!' Burt sounded almost triumphant. 'Look . . .' He pointed to a group of wildebeest who were standing, staring at them. 'How long . . . how much longer will you be here?' he asked suddenly.

As this was a question she had been asking herself, Rayanne should have known the answer, she thought, but she didn't.

'I haven't a clue,' she said honestly.

She turned away, looking at the veld with its strange umbrella-shaped trees, the groups of bushes and the glimpses of wild animals that she saw now as quite normal, no longer getting wildly excited when the saw a cheetah or a wildebeest.

'How long were you invited for?' Burt, deftly driving round a rut in the earth road, asked.

'No time was mentioned. I was asked to come and stay to give me the chance to study wild life conservation. I imagine I can stay as long as I like,' she said, her voice worried. 'So Mrs Jefferson says.'

'But Mrs Jefferson isn't the real boss,' Burt pointed out.

He swerved as a warthog ran across the road, and slowed up as the family followed, a wife, and several small ones, all with their little tails pointed up skywards.

'How long are *you* staying?' Rayanne asked.

He shrugged. 'Any moment now I must go. I've several jobs waiting for me and I can't postpone them for ever. I've got my notes and photographs and when I've put the lot together, I'll send it to Cary to see if he'll write a foreword for it.'

'I'll miss you,' Rayanne said impulsively, and again wished she hadn't, for Burt turned and gave her such a sweet smile that she felt absolutely mean. It was cruel to let him think

147

she felt more for him than just affection.

Ahead of them was the game warden's fenced-in house. There were several Rovers and big trucks with crates on them waiting. Burt parked his Rover and they went into the house. Cary was standing drinking coffee, he looked at them and gave a casual nod.

Rayanne stared at him. How handsome he was, so tall and straight, so lean and strong. Somehow his khaki shirt and trousers made him look even more handsome, as did the big hat he had perched on the back of his head. As if he could read her thoughts, he lifted it off, gave her a grin and tossed the hat on the table.

'Come and meet everyone, Ray . . . and Burt, too, of course,' he said. His arm lightly round Rayanne's shoulders, he took her round the room, introducing her.

There were so many names it was useless to try to remember them all, Rayanne decided. The biologist who would do the shooting was a tall, big-built man with greying hair and a sunburned skin. His son, Keith Bilkington, was with him. Then there were several vets and game catchers, who apparently went from reserve to reserve when needed. There was a lot of noise as the room was not large and there were many of them, but Cary seemed to go out of his way to look after her, getting her coffee, and even a chair Then he looked down at her.

'You're coming with me. Okay?'

She nodded. 'Okay.'

'I thought it would be best,' Cary said, 'as my mother is so anxious about you.'

Rayanne's mouth twisted a little wryly. 'Very thoughtful of you, I'm sure.'

'You'll excuse me if I mix a bit? I want to talk to Dr Bilkington.'

'Of course.' Sipping the hot strong coffee, Rayanne looked around. Burt was making notes of something the biologist, Paul Bilkington, was telling him. Then Keith, the son, came and squatted on the ground by Rayanne's side.

'How come a dolly like you is here?' he asked, with a grin. A friendly pleasant boy, she thought at once, about her own age.

'I'm supposed to be writing a thesis on wild life conservation.'

He whistled softly. 'So with good looks, brains do go too, sometimes. How is the thesis going?'

'Not very well,' Rayanne admitted. 'You see, I came as a sceptic, feeling the money spent on all this should be spent on starving people. I'm still not sure how I really feel about it, but I'm beginning to realise the importance of conservation.'

Keith, with his short blond hair and suntanned skin, chuckled.

'Well, I bet you have it all stuffed down your throat. I reckon Jefferson never talks of anything else.'

149

'Oh, he does,' she said quickly, and saw the grin on Keith's face. 'Sometimes,' she added.

'Well, he'd have to be a bit of a fool never to talk of anything else to someone dishy as you. Who are you driving with? I'm afraid I can't ask you as I'm going with Dad. We're doing the shooting, you see. The others do the manual work.' He laughed. 'Sooner them than me! One thing, the hippos are so dopey you can make them do almost anything. Oh, Dad's waving at me, so we've to get going.' He smiled at Rayanne. 'Nice to have met you. Didn't expect such a dolly in the bush. Maybe we'll meet again?'

'Maybe,' said Rayanne, suddenly realising just what a boy he was! Funny how much more mature girls in their early twenties were than men. She much preferred older men, men in their thirties, like Cary . . .

Cary! If only she had never met Cary . . . the heartbreak that she knew lay ahead of her was really frightening. Wasn't she being a fool, she asked herself, to stay on? Surely the longer she was near him, the harder it would be to go? Yet she dreaded the thought of leaving.

'Ray!' Cary called. 'Ready?'

'Ready!' she called back, and hurried to his side. Walking to the Rover, he told her briefly what was going to happen.

'We round up the herds and seek out the ones we want. Dr Bilkington is our adviser as well as shooter. He'll go ahead. Then we race

150

after the sleepy animals and when they really collapse, the Africans can handle them, with our aid, of course. The vets will give each animal a quick examination, because we don't want to cart off sick ones.'

'Why are they being shipped to England?'

Because there's always the danger that some disease will come along or something happen so that they all die or get killed and no longer exist. We're sending animals to zoos all over the world to ensure that they're not wiped out.'

In the Rover both were silent as they drove out of the fenced-in garden and were in the reserve. There was one Rover ahead . . . that must be Dr Bilkington and Keith, his son.

'What did you think of young Bilkington?' Cary asked. 'I saw him talking to you.'

She laughed. 'He was paying me idiotic compliments. He must be mad to think I believed them even for a moment.'

'What sort of compliments?'

'Well . . .' She hesitated, 'rather immature. Kept calling me a *dolly* . . . oh, and he told me I was dishy and . . . I remember now, he said that *so with good looks, brains do go too, sometimes.* Cheeky, that's what he was,' she said scornfully.

'Would you have preferred it had he told you that he found you a real old bag? Hideous, dumb, and dull?' Cary asked gravely.

Bumping about in the Rover, Rayanne looked at him. She saw he was trying not to

151

laugh. Suddenly she was laughing and he turned to look at her, obviously glad he could laugh now.

'Of course I didn't,' she managed to say.

Cary shrugged. 'Let's face it, Ray, you're a difficult person. One hesitates to approach you in case one says the wrong thing.'

'*I'm* difficult? Why, it's . . .' Rayanne began, and stopped, for Cary was laughing again.

'Never,' he said, 'never in my life have I known a girl like you. One only has to open one's mouth and you're on the offensive, or perhaps I should say the defensive.'

'I am . . .' she began indignantly and again stopped, frowning as she looked at him. 'Am I?'

'Are you? That's no lie,' he said, and swung off the earth road, the Rover bumping over the veld, brushing by the large bushes that seemed determined to mass together and stop them from moving.

Now the Rovers had separated as if searching for something. There was a two-way radio that occasionally produced a voice, saying the hippos had not yet been found.

'It's ridiculous,' Cary said impatiently. 'I sent guides out at dawn to trace them and they said there were several herds here.'

Ahead of them a herd of enormous elephants were making their slow way to a small dam. Cary slowed up and then one of the elephants turned his head in their direction,

152

slowly swinging his trunk, his eyes thoughtful or—so they seemed to Rayanne—rather ominously thoughtful, she decided, his great ears went back. He stood still, staring at the Rover that had come to a halt, and suddenly the elephant let out a dreadful scream.

Cary got into reverse and the Rover leapt backwards as he twisted and turned the steering wheel, guiding them through the mass of bushes.

The elephant began to move as if to follow them, swinging his trunk, then seemed to change his mind, almost shrugging his shoulders and following the other elephants who had taken no notice of what he was doing.

Rayanne felt her whole body relaxing. Cary went on reversing, his body turned round as he deftly guided the Rover through the bushes. Finally he slowed up and stopped. Then he spoke into the two-way radio, advising the other drivers of the enraged elephant.

'May be injured,' he said. 'Reckon young Wallace could cope. He's got a crossbow with him, only it might mess things up if the elephant goes berserk.'

An answer came back from Dick Wallace and Cary turned finally to Rayanne.

'Well?' he asked cheerfully. 'Hope you weren't too scared.'

'Scared?' She tried to laugh, but even her voice was unsteady. Never had she been so terrified in her life—that great huge creature

153

screaming his hatred of them, moving threateningly towards them. He could have smashed the Rover and everything in it almost in seconds.

'You'll get used to it,' Cary said cheerfully, manoeuvring the Rover around. 'So long as the car doesn't stall, you're okay. Ah!'

A message came over the radio. The hippos had been traced. Directions were given as to how to get to them.

Cary nodded happily. 'Now we go slowly until we see them . . .'

'Why?'

'We don't want them racing off before we're there. You wouldn't like to back out, Ray?' he asked suddenly. 'You're very white.'

She turned quickly to look at him. 'I bet you were the first time an elephant screamed at you. Of course I don't want to back out. I'm enjoying this . . . it's . . . it's . . . well, it's different,' she finished lamely.

'I'll say! Very different from your safe little life in London.'

'Safe? With all that traffic?' Rayanne laughed. 'It's not different in that way.'

'Sure you feel safe with me?' Cary asked suddenly. 'You wouldn't have preferred to go with Burt?'

'Of course I feel safe with you.' Puzzled, Rayanne stared at him. How he liked to throw unexpected questions at her, she thought. 'Why should I prefer to be with Burt?'

154

'I just wondered. You seem to rather fancy him,' Cary said casually, looking at his watch and frowning. 'You've quite got my poor mother worried about it.'

'Why should she worry?'

Cary chuckled. 'Well, as you know she's decided that you're to be my bride.'

'What absolute nonsense!' Rayanne's cheeks burned, her eyes flashed, her hands clenched. Just how much more of this could she stand? she asked herself. 'As if I'd marry you if you asked me!' she said angrily, for attack was the best defence, her father had once said.

Cary laughed. 'Wouldn't you?' he asked, and suddenly the Rover shot forward, causing Rayanne to slide down the seat bumping into him. 'Steady on,' he warned. 'No time for battles, now . . . there are the hippos!'

*   *   *

The rest of the day was too exciting for Rayanne to have time to feel furious with Cary for what he had said. They had rounded the hippos and Dr Bilkington had doped the one he advised, the hippo had raced away, but slowly his or her running had slowed until finally it was a sort of drunken walk, with frequent stumbles and a final collapse. Then the veterinary surgeons had got to work, examining the animal quickly, passing him

155

or her or saying they did not advise it. The little wound was treated with a disinfectant and those allowed to go back to freedom were given another injection which, with amazing speed, brought them back to normal. Meanwhile the staff were driving, slowly and with patience, the huge ungainly chosen animals into the trucks.

Later Cary drove Rayanne to see the elephant that had taken a dislike to them. He was lying on his side, still unconscious, with Dick Wallace working on him. The elephant was obviously badly injured.

'Not to worry,' Dick Wallace said, seeing Rayanne's look of dismay. 'It's fortunate you saw him and we found him. He must have been in terrible pain, no wonder he hated everyone he saw.'

'Will you be able to cure him?' Rayanne asked.

Dick Wallace shrugged. 'I reckon so. These are tough creatures, but I'm taking him back with me and keeping him under sedation to make sure the wounds heal.'

It was a long tiring day and as Cary drove her home, Rayanne yawned. Cary, who had been rather silent, looked at her.

'Well, was it worth while?'

She smiled in the middle of another yawn. 'It was absolutely marvellous.' She yawned. I'm sorry about this, but I am sleepy, I'm afraid.'

'A hot bath and an early night,' Cary

suggested. 'By the way, I hope this will have helped your work on your thesis. You don't seem to be getting on with it.'

Rayanne caught her breath. Was this another hint that she was not wanted?

'I'm getting on with it all right,' she said quickly, though she knew it was a lie. 'I've got copious notes. It's just a matter . . .'

'Of knowing from which angle to write,' Cary mimicked her voice. 'You've told me that before. Well, has today given you that angle?'

Rayanne clasped her hands together tightly and stared ahead. It was lovely countryside, yet she was giving it so little attention.

'I'm not sure,' she said slowly. Had it? Was it perhaps the importance of having found the elephant who was in pain and therefore a menace to all living creatures? Was it watching the vets as they handled the animals? They all seemed to believe their jobs were worth doing.

'Is it because you're not interested,' Cary asked, 'or just that you feel inarticulate?'

Rayanne frowned. She recognised some of the landmarks around her—a huge rock, carved out by generations of rain and wind into looking like a lion's head; a cluster of cypress trees which seemed out of place here in the bush, but a few clumps of bricks piled up told the sad story of the house that had once been there and probably burned in a fire. These meant they were nearly home and the questions would cease.

'I honestly don't know,' she admitted. 'I'm interested, very interested. I was a bit sceptical at first, but now I'm beginning to understand how important it is. I just can't seem to find . . .' She paused, her cheeks hot. 'You must be bored stiff hearing me say that.'

They were going through the last gate, Cary shouting to the African who opened it and who replied with a big grin and a salute.

'At least,' Cary said as he drove surprisingly fast down the drive, 'you're honest.'

Then they were there and Mrs Jefferson came to meet them. 'My dear child, you do look tired! Was it very frightening? You wouldn't get me going out like that. Why, those elephants . . .'

Finally Cary left them and Rayanne had her bath, a little sleep, and woke refreshed. She shuffled through the notes she had made. What should she write about? Perhaps if she made a skeleton draft . . . what did conservation teach the civilised world? Did the understanding, or partial understanding, of the migratory habits of certain animals really teach the civilised world anything worth knowing? she wondered. Was it important to keep the wild animals alive? Was it really necessary?

Perhaps if she answered those questions, it would get her started, she thought.

Later that evening, she excused herself and went to bed early. But not to sleep. Instead she sat by the small table and sorted out her notes.

Somehow or other the thesis must be written.

During the next few days, she worked on her notes, trying different angles, unable to write anything that she thought was worth even reading. She began to feel even more depressed, for it showed that her brothers might be right. Perhaps she had no brains, after all?

Cary had gone away, suddenly called by an urgent phone message. He didn't say where he had gone, but Burt made a guess that it was to help Aileen.

'He likes to play the cool indifferent dedicated man, but I think he really fell for Aileen,' Burt said with a chuckle.

The course was nearing its end, soon the noisy students would be returning to their home towns and a few weeks of quietness would follow, Mrs Jefferson said.

'Not that I mind having them around. They keep to their own quarters, but I do get a bit tired of the noise their transistors make. Do they really have to have such loud music?' she asked Rayanne.

It was Burt who answered. 'Sure they do, Mrs Jefferson. That's the only way to be part of the music.' He grinned as he spoke. 'At least, that's what they say. They have to be a *part* so the noise must screech through the brain, leaving you stunned.'

'A funny way to enjoy music,' Mrs Jefferson commented.

He lifted a finger. 'I agree, but . . . ah I we're not young, Mrs Jefferson.' He turned to Rayanne who was standing by the window, watching the movements on the sand as the crocodiles came slowly out of the water. How she would miss the crocodiles . . .

She swung round. 'What? Sorry, I didn't hear you.'

'You're young, my dear,' Mrs Jefferson said gently. 'D'you like loud music?'

'Loud music?' Rayanne's face wrinkled as she frowned. 'Well, I don't know, but I do like to *hear* it. I mean, there's no point in listening to it if it's too soft, is there?'

She wondered why they both laughed. 'I can't see the joke.'

'Ah, my dear child,' Mrs Jefferson said with a smile, 'there isn't a joke—it's just that the different generations see everything so differently.' She looked up at. Burt. 'How old are you? I'd have thought you were one of the young ones.'

He bowed. 'Thank you, madame. Thank you very much. I'll never see thirty-five again, I'm going on fast towards forty so I can't be called young.'

'That's not old, Burt. Cary is just thirty-five,' Mrs Jefferson said.

'I think men in their mid-thirties are the most interesting of all,' said Rayanne. 'I met Keith that day we got the hippos and I found him awfully boring, and he's about my age.'

Burt bowed towards her. 'You've made my day, if I may be so corny. What a comforting thought to a man as the years race by! Do you honestly think we grow more attractive the older we grow?'

Rayanne laughed. 'Depends on how much older you do grow.'

Later that day as Burt patiently taught her to drive the Land Rover, he asked her:

'Did you really find Keith a bore?'

Rayanne was concentrating on what had to be done. They were driving outside the game reserve on a rather bad road but with little traffic. 'He was terribly immature.'

'You prefer mature men?'

'Who doesn't?' she said as she deftly turned a corner.

'How's it going? Feeling happier?'

'Much,' Rayanne smiled. 'Thanks to your patience.'

'Does Cary know I'm teaching you?'

'I . . . well, I suppose he doesn't. I didn't tell him. Did you?'

'Of course not. I was afraid he'd insist on teaching you himself and I knew it would be an absolute flop. The things you need most, Rayanne, are praise, encouragement and . . .'

'Patience,' Rayanne finished. Thanks to you, I've had all three.'

'My pleasure,' he said, and laughed. 'Why do you want to drive, Rayanne?'

'So that when I get home I can buy a car and

show my brothers that I can drive.'

'So you are going home?' he asked, his voice becoming grave.

'Of course.' She turned to stare at him and Burt grabbed at the wheel, just managing to save them from going off sideways into the deep ditch.

'Hey, watch it, young woman!' he said gruffly.

'Then don't talk to me,' she told him in return.

Back at the house, they found Mrs Jefferson in great distress.

'If only Cary was here! He'd cope with it. He can manage anything and anyone . . .'

'What's the trouble?' Burt asked. 'Maybe I can help.'

'I've just heard. Samantha has left Mike!'

'I don't believe it,' Rayanne said quickly. 'She wouldn't do a thing like that, I'm sure.'

'Well, Sister Macintyre was here earlier. She wanted to speak to you, Rayanne. She seems to think it's all your fault.' Mrs Jefferson, sitting down in her deep armchair, pressed her hands together, her face unhappy. 'I told her I was sure it wasn't, but she wouldn't believe me. I don't think she likes you.'

'How could it be my fault?'

'She says you've made Samantha restless and discontented and . . .'

'She was like that before I got here. Samantha knows I can't really understand why

162

she's so miserable. Yet I can, in a way. If only Mike could interest her in his work!'

'Or give her a baby,' said Burt. 'That's the real trouble, I think.'

Rayanne pressed her hands to her mouth, her eyes widening as she thought of something. But perhaps, she thought, it was better to say nothing at this stage.

'What's Mike doing?' she asked.

'What can he do? She went off . . .'

'She can't drive,' Rayanne said.

'I gather she got Kwido. You weren't using him, so he took her to Perlee and she told him she was staying with some friends, so when he came back, he concluded that Mike would know and said nothing.'

'Then where does Daphne Macintyre come into this?' Burt asked.

'It seems she went to see Samantha because she was worried about her. Samantha's had a bad cold for some time and . . . well, she was out. Daphne waited and Mike came in and knew nothing about it. Then he sent for Kwido, and . . . well, she's just gone.'

'I'm sure she hasn't. Perhaps Mike has forgotten she was going away. He's so lost in his work that he could forget anything.'

'I hope you're right, Rayanne. I do feel so upset about it. Cary won't be at all pleased . . .'

'Well,' said Burt, 'we can't do anything to help, I'm afraid. I think I'll go have a shower. You, too, Rayanne?'

163

'Yes, I am rather sticky with dust,' Rayanne said.

Should she phone Mike? she wondered. Where was he? Had he driven to Perlee looking for her? Samantha wouldn't run away. She just wasn't that sort. She might have a terrific quarrel, but it would all be open.

Suddenly Rayanne had an idea . . . Very quietly she made her way outside, knowing Burt must still be having his shower and that Mrs Jefferson would think nothing of the sound of a car starting up. Luckily the key was left in it as it was always left there, since there were no burglars to fear.

A little nervous, because she had only had a few lessons from Burt, Rayanne started up the engine. All went well, for with no traffic around, one could take a corner badly and yet be quite safe. The African at the gate looked a bit surprised, but let her through, and she drove towards the Crisps' gate. There she paused and asked Lobitha if he knew where the master was.

'He has gone to the Clinic and will then go to Perlee,' Lobitha told her.

'Oh dear!' Rayanne said, and thought quickly. Well, she had better go to the Clinic, though she had no desire for a scene with Daphne Macintyre, but if Mike could be seen before he left for Perlee . . .'

It wasn't easy and she wondered if Lobitha was amused by her antics, but she finally

164

managed to reverse and turn round, making along the road for the Clinic. Suddenly she saw a deep furrow in the road and swung sideways to avoid it, jamming on the brakes. The engine stopped.

She tried to start it again. It refused. She tried and tried, for the night was beginning to come down and she was on a lonely back road, one rarely used, she knew. Somewhere an owl howled . . . she heard the chattering of the monkeys who usually went to bed early because they feared the dark. She tried the engine again and again and it refused to start . . .

Should she get out and look at the engine? she wondered. What good would that do? She knew nothing about engines. Should she press on the hooter perhaps doing a S.O.S. sound. If Burt heard and found the Rover gone, he would come to look for her. But could he hear? The road was some way from the house. But surely he would miss her soon . . . well, at least within the next hour, and come and look for her.

Suddenly she caught her breath. Coming through the bushes towards her were several elephants, pulling down branches, eating as if famished. She sat very still, hoping that the sight of a Rover was so familiar that they would take no notice. So long as there wasn't one that had been hurt, she thought, and felt the sweat of fear break out on her face and

165

down her back.

They came very slowly and walked round the Rover. She closed her eyes tightly and said a little prayer. She could hear the sound of their slow heavy steps, the crash of branches of leaves torn down, and then it seemed to recede . . .

Opening her eyes, she saw that they had gone past her. They had ignored the Rover! She could feel the tension leave her body and she flopped in her seat. Glancing in the mirror, she saw the elephants had vanished. Instead a car was driving towards her . . .

Cary!

He drew up behind her and walked to her side. She looked up at him. How angry he would be! She had done the very thing he had forbidden.

'Those elephants pass here?' he asked curtly.

'Yes,' she nodded, her throat seeming to close up so that speech was impossible.

'You must have been frightened.'

'I . . . I was.' She swallowed. He had every right to be angry with her. She had been stupid to come out alone.

'What's wrong?' he asked.

'She stalled, and I can't start the engine.'

'Well, come back with me and I'll send one of the mechanics down.' He opened the door and helped her out. As they walked back to his car, he spoke again. 'What were you doing?'

She looked up anxiously. 'I wanted to catch Mike before he left for Perlee. Lobitha told me Mike had gone to the Clinic and then was going on to the town. I wanted to stop him.'

'Why?' he asked as he started the engine and carefully reversed the car until he could find a flat part of the earth road that allowed him to turn.

'Because I'm sure Samantha will phone him tonight.'

'You know why Samantha went? You knew she was going?'

'No, I most certainly didn't.' Rayanne twisted on the seat to look at him. 'I had no idea at all. In fact, I'm sure she must have left a note for him. She wouldn't do such a thing.'

'Why didn't she tell him? Why leave a note?'

'Because they've been arguing about it and I think she was afraid of a big row . . .'

'How come you know so much about it all? Sister Macintyre . . .'

Rayanne's cheeks were hot. 'If you prefer to believe Daphne Macintyre, I can't stop you. She just wants to make trouble for me. I only know about it because Samantha discussed it with me. She wants to adopt a child, but Mike doesn't. But she thought if she could have a baby on trial . . . you know, just for a few months, he might change his mind.'

'Baby on trial?' Cary echoed. 'Sounds odd.'

'It isn't odd at all. I think it's very sensible.

Lots of people want babies, but when they get them and find they cry and have to be fed every four hours and so on, they no longer want them. The reverse can also occur. Mike might find what fun it was to have a baby to love and look after, so Samantha was going to try to be a foster-mother. She thought that way Mike might change his mind—also if they're successful foster-parents, it might help them if they applied for a child they could adopt.'

'I see. So Samantha went in to collect the baby?'

'Oh no, you can't do things as fast as that. She couldn't phone them, because Mike might walk in at any moment and she didn't want a big row, so she thought she'd go and stay there for a night or two and see what could be arranged. I'm sure she must have left a note for Mike.'

'Well, he says, she didn't.'

'But Daphne Macintyre was at the house before him,' said Rayanne.

Cary frowned. 'Are you suggesting Sister Macintyre would hide the note?'

'She's capable of anything as far as I'm concerned,' Rayanne said bitterly. 'She and Christine both hate me. They snub me, ignore me, do everything they can to make life unpleasant for me.'

'I think you're being rather melodramatic,' Cary said coldly.

'I am not,' she began angrily, and paused.

168

'How did you come to find me?'

'I'd just arrived home and Mother was getting worried because you weren't in your room. Then Burt found the Rover had gone. He went off to look for you, but I decided to see Mike first.'

'Of course, he has priority,' said Rayanne. 'It didn't matter what happened to me!'

He looked sideways at her. 'You had asked for it, you know. It was a stupid thing to do.'

'I know, but . . . well, I'd only expected to go to Mike's. That would have been quite safe.'

'Not really. No more safe than here.'

Rayanne was silent, twisting her fingers together, wondering when he would really get angry with her for what she had done. Perhaps he would seize it as a good reason for telling her it was time she left Jefferson Hall. That she had outstayed her welcome—if welcome she had ever been as far as he was concerned.

Back at the house, Mrs Jefferson was nearly in tears, but Cary said they had phone calls to make.

'Come with me, Rayanne,' he told her, leading the way to his library. He put the call through to the Clinic. Mike had gone! 'Sister Macintyre,' he said, his voice cold, 'you're sure there was no message left in the Crisps' house? No letter? What . . . oh, I see. Naturally you didn't look. But you didn't see one that might have been there and perhaps blown on the floor because of a draught through an open window? What . . . oh, I see. The windows were open, so it might have happened. I understand. I quite realise that had you seen such a letter, you would have told Mike about it. Naturally. Thank you, Sister Macintyre.' He put down the receiver and looked at Rayanne.

'Well, she says she didn't see a letter or note.'

'She says!' Rayanne said, her voice bitter. 'Well, it all boils down to this: you either believe her or you believe me. We'll see what Samantha says. Have you quite finished with me? I feel like a hot bath.'

'Yes, quite. I expect you do.'

At the door, Rayanne hesitated, then she turned. 'Cary—' she began.

He looked up from some papers he was sorting out.

'Yes?' It was a cold *yes,* an uninviting one that made it even harder to do what she felt she ought.

'I'm sorry,' she said. 'I shouldn't have taken the Rover out alone. It was just that I was upset. I . . I was surprised that you weren't angry with me. I . . . I . . .'

'Thought I'd be a monster as I usually am, like all men?' His words were clipped sharp and short as if he was angry. 'I said nothing to you because I knew you'd been punished enough when those elephants went by you. It must have been a bad moment, but look, Ray, it's time we cleared up something.' He

170

put down the papers and walked towards her slowly. 'Let's get this straight. Why have you this hatred of men? You hate me, I know that. Do you hate Burt? Did you hate Keith? What is it that upsets you? I've an idea that you're afraid of us. Every time a man speaks to you, you clench your hands, stiffen your body. Surely it can't just be your brothers that have given you this complex?'

She looked up at him. 'I . . . I don't know.' I've always felt like this. I think it was my brothers always teasing me, treating me as a little girl even when I was nineteen . . . even now,' she added bitterly. 'They just won't accept me as I am. Then . . . then nothing I ever did was right in Dad's eyes. I wanted him to be proud of me. He's terribly proud of . . . of the others. I . . . began to feel it was all so hopeless, that nothing I could ever do would please him, yet it was the most important thing in the world to me : to make him proud of his only daughter.' She turned away. 'I suppose . . . I suppose I see all men as my enemies as a result. I feel every time that I'm about to do battle with them, that they're against me before I even open my mouth.'

'I see.' Cary's voice was thoughtful. 'I wonder how we can cure you.'

'I don't . . . don't think there's any cure. I'll never be famous, and . . . and . . .' She jerked open the door and ran down the corridor, but not before Cary had seen the tears running down her cheeks.

CHAPTER EIGHT

After a sleepless unhappy night, Rayanne
woke very early. She showered and dressed,
suddenly feeling the walls of the room closing
in on her threateningly, like those of a prison.
Cary's refusal to believe her hurt her more
than anything that had ever happened. If he
preferred to believe Daphne Macintyre . . .

It had been a strange evening. After
Cary had driven her back to the house, Mrs
Jefferson had burst into tears as she took
Rayanne in her arms.

'My dear child, I was so frightened for you
. . .'

And then Burt had phoned to find out if
there was any news of Rayanne and when
told she was safely there, had slammed down
the receiver—according to Cary, who told
Rayanne, a slightly sarcastic smile playing
round his mouth.

Then Mrs Jefferson had startled them by
announcing that she had invited a few people
to dinner but that no one need go, if they
desired not to. She had stood there, this little
loving woman who had made Rayanne feel, for
once, that someone cared about her.

'But I hope you'll feel well enough to come,

Rayanne,' Mrs Jefferson had said wistfully.

Cary had strode across the room, tugging at the lobe of his left ear. 'Who have you asked?'

Mrs Jefferson held up her hand, and ticked off each guest on her fingers. 'Christine, Daphne . . .'

Cary had swung round, looking across the room at Rayanne, his eyes mocking as if in challenge.

'Of course I'll come.'

'And I will, too,' Rayanne said at once, stiffening, feeling that shiver slide down her back.

Mrs Jefferson beamed, 'I'm so glad. Then there's . . .' she had named two of the vets, and added: 'Oh, and Keith Bilkington. He phoned up to speak to you, Rayanne dear, and when I said you were out, he sounded so disappointed I asked him to dinner. I hope you don't mind?' She looked anxious.

'Of course she doesn't,' Cary had interrupted, giving Rayanne no chance to speak. 'Keith fell for her heavily.' He sounded amused, moving with his long effortless strides towards the door.

'He didn't. It's just his way . . .' Rayanne had begun, when Burt came almost pounding in, hardly seeing Cary, as he brushed past him and made straight for Rayanne.

His hands on her shoulders, he shook her. 'I thought . . . well, I didn't dare think.' His voice was harsh. 'I . . . What happened?'

173

Cary stood still in the doorway, looking amused.

'She was looking for Mike and the engine stalled. Apparently you didn't teach her how to cope with such a problem.'

'The car stalled?' Burt's fingers were digging into Rayanne's skin. She saw the shock that showed so plainly on his face.

'Yes—and little Ray had some elephants walk past her. Punishment enough for her foolishness, so stop being so melodramatic, Burt. It won't get you anywhere,' Cary said curtly, and left the room.

Burt's hands had fallen to his side. 'Were you scared?'

Rayanne managed a poor imitation of a laugh. 'It was rather terrifying. Luckily they were in good tempers.'

'Why were you looking for Mike?'

So she had told him, aware that Mrs Jefferson had quietly left the room as if not wanting to disturb them, what had happened.

'And Cary won't believe me. I'm sure Samantha would have left a note. I wanted to tell Mike that I thought Samantha had gone to find out about foster-mothering a baby. I didn't want him to be worried about her,' Rayanne had finished.

'Was it that important?'

Rayanne nodded. 'To me, it was. Besides, I only meant to go to the Clinic, and that's not very far.'

174

'Nevertheless the road goes through the Reserve and it's wisest not to go alone. Was Cary furious when he found you?'

Rayanne laughed, a real laugh this time—at herself.

'I thought he would be—in fact, I was quite scared, for he was right and I was in the wrong, but it didn't seem to have worried him at all. He said my fear was punishment enough . . . he meant fear of the elephants.'

'It was fear of him?' Burt had asked, his voice changing, becoming a little aggressive. 'You're not really afraid of him, are you?'

'Well . . .' Rayanne had hesitated. 'Not really afraid, but I am here on . . . well, he let me come because of Uncle Joe and the least I can do really is to . . . well, to conform with his regulations. And now we've got this party tonight.'

'What party?' Burt had asked, so she had told him. He had looked annoyed.

'Still, it might be best for you, or else you may dream of elephants.' Then his hands had taken hold of her shoulders; this time more gently. 'Rayanne, there's something I must tell you . . .' he began, and Rayanne had known the moment she feared was there.

Burt loved her and was going to tell her—which meant that she would have to hurt him with the truth. She had felt her body stiffen as she waited. 'It was that moment when the door had opened and Cary stood there. He stared at them, looking puzzled.

'Sorry if I interrupted something,' he said curtly, giving Rayanne an odd look and quickly closing the door so that they were alone. But Rayanne had moved and Burt's hands dropped. He was scowling, 'Never get a moment to ourselves in this house!'

Rayanne had seized her chance of escape. 'I must go and change,' she had said, and almost ran down the corridor to her room.

She had been careful not to join the others until the guests had come. She wore a white sheath dress with a green belt, and a green ribbon round her head. As she quietly joined the guests, Keith made for her.

'Hi . . . I told you we'd meet again,' he said almost triumphantly.

* * *

It had been a difficult evening, Rayanne was thinking this next day as she walked down the well-cared-for lawn towards the muddy river. Daphne Macintyre at the party had looked like a cat with a saucer of cream; a corny expression, yet it was true. She had not spoken to Rayanne, but had obviously ignored her, almost to a point of rudeness. So had Christine, for that matter, but with Christine it had been even worse. For Cary had never left Christine's side, while Rayanne had been unable to throw off Keith, who followed her

176

round like a lost sheep, and Burt, who kept asking her to dance, whisking her away from Keith.

It had been a relief, or so Rayanne had thought at the time, when she was able to slip away to bed. But then the real troubles had begun.

Just how much longer could she stay in this, to her at least, paradise? she had asked herself. How long would she be welcome? By Cary, that was. She was sure he had been angry because she had gone off on her own in the Rover; also he had obviously preferred to believe Daphne Macintyre rather than Rayanne Briscoe! Then he had seen Burt upset and angry—and must have realised he had interrupted them at an important moment, and then finally his total avoidance of her during the whole evening. Not once, not even once, had he danced with her! Wouldn't it be better, she had asked herself, tossing and turning restlessly in bed, if she left? More dignified? More . . . more . . . she couldn't find the right word and then the tears had come. Foolish, no-good tears because she loved him so much and if she went, might never see him again. How could she do it?

Now as she turned away from the river she had strolled down to, she saw little Dorcas, the African maid who looked after her, come running, holding a note.

'I could not find you . . . you were not

in bed,' she said almost accusingly. 'He is waiting.'

'Thanks.' Rayanne took the note in her hands and, recognising Cary's handwriting, felt fear slide down her back. Cary had something important to tell her? It could only be . . . it must be . . .

The equivalent of dismissal was an expression her father often used, and somehow it seemed to fit this perfectly. After a good night's sleep, Cary must have decided that Rayanne's disobedience of his regulations could only mean one thing: that she was *unsuitable for the environment,* another of her father's favourite expressions. She wondered why she was thinking of her father . . . was it because this would disappoint him still more? That if she was packed off from here, he would have to admit again that he had a strange daughter?

'*The runt of the litter,*' she had heard him say once. She had been much younger and had fled to her bedroom in tears. Later her mother had tried to explain that it hadn't been said seriously, that it was a joke . . . But it hadn't been a joke in Rayanne's eyes, nor would it ever be.

Now she turned the envelope over several times. She was afraid to open it. It was like receiving a death warrant—for if she left here, life would no longer have any reason. Life without Cary would be . . . nothing. Yet that was what life was bound to be, she knew.

178

Opening the envelope, she was shocked to see her hands trembling. Was she showing her emotion so plainly? Would it be a tactful brush-off? she wondered. Something like 'I feel sure you have collected enough notes and may find it easier to write the thesis in your own home.' A polite way of saying: 'Get out!'

She read the note. It was brief and to the point. 'Please come immediately to my study as I have something important to tell you.'

Come immediately—and Dorcas had been looking for her, Rayanne realised, so goodness only knew how long Cary had been waiting. This would only add to his displeasure, his certainty that the 'headache girl' must go.

She hurried indoors, not bothering to look in the mirror, for there was no sense in that since he never really saw her, and tapped on his door.

'Come in,' he said impatiently.

Rayanne obeyed, closing the door and leaning against it, as she stared at the man behind the desk. Cary was standing, not looking up as he sorted out some papers with a frown on his face.

'It took you a long time,' he commented.

'I'm sorry. Dorcas couldn't find me. I was in the garden.'

Cary looked up, his dark tufty eyebrows moving.

'You had a rendezvous?' he asked sarcastically. She coloured, knowing he was thinking of Burt.

'No. Just thinking that perhaps I . . .' She drew a deep breath. This was the right moment, the moment to tell him she knew she should go home.

'Sit down, then, and don't look scared to death. I'm not going to eat you,' Cary said irritably, going on sorting out the papers. 'What were you thinking of, looking at the crocs?'

'Just . . . well . . .' This was something she couldn't tell him, for it was the truth. She had been thinking of him and how desolate her life would be when he walked out of it. 'I wondered what you wanted to see me about. What have I done wrong this time?' she asked almost defiantly.

He stood up, putting the papers on one side, and stared at her. 'Rayanne Briscoe, isn't it time you grew up? Stop harping on that martyr line. You haven't done anything wrong. In any case, that's not why I sent for you.' He looked at his watch. 'There isn't time for this ridiculous . . . Look, in ten minutes I have to be on my way to New York.'

'New York?' Rayanne was startled.

'Yes, and I need your help.'

'My . . . my help?' Rayanne's eyes widened as she stared at him. Cary was asking for *her* help! She found it hard to believe.

But it was true, and he sounded really worried as he went on:

180

'Yes. You see, this has come quite by surprise, just as my trip to Cape Town was. I can usually avoid these journeys during the courses here, but this time I've failed. As you know, there have been far fewer lectures than there should have been because of my Cape Town visit, and I had planned to wind up everything this afternoon.' He patted the pile of papers by his side. 'These are notes on previous talks I've given and a rough draft of how to tie up all the bits, but—and this is the important part, Ray—most of the lecture must be *ad lib*. The students are uninterested as soon as you start reading and it's important for them to leave here understanding why we support wild life conservation and what this reserve is for.' He paused, then smiled. 'I want you to give the lecture.'

Had he slapped her face, she could hardly have been more shocked. 'Me?' she almost howled with surprise. 'But . . .'

He stood up, glancing at his watch again. 'There are the notes, Ray. Mike will give you any information you need. I expect you have plenty yourself that you've collected for your thesis. Use the personal touch. Tell the students you came here as a sceptic. You were, weren't you? Perhaps you still are, but tell them what you've learned, what has caught your interest. But why tell you, I know you'll manage all right.'

Striding to the door, Cary smiled at her.

Somehow Rayanne jerked herself into action. She had felt, for a moment, stunned.

'But wouldn't Christine be better? I mean, she's been here longer than me and . . .' she began.

Cary's hand was on the door knob. 'Christine's bright in the laboratory but hopeless when it comes to facts about conservation.' He opened the door, then turned and said casually: 'By the way, you were quite right. Mike phoned me and said Samantha told him she had left a note for him.' Cary closed the door and was gone.

Clutching the papers, Rayanne made her way to her bedroom. She put them on the table, all her movements slow as if the slightest effort was exhausting. She could not believe it. Cary had asked her to take his place before his soon-leaving students.

Somehow she moved to join the others at breakfast. Mrs Jefferson leapt to her feet.

'Dear child, what has happened? You look so white,' she said anxiously.

Rayanne managed a weak smile. 'Cary has asked me to lecture the students this afternoon.'

'So what?' Burt asked irritably. 'If he can do it, so can you.'

'But, Burt,' Rayanne almost wailed, 'I know hardly anything about it.'

'Neither do they. You must have lectured before.'

182

'I have—but not here.' Rayanne sounded desperate. 'I just . . .'

'And what's so different about here?' Burt asked, his voice suddenly cold. 'It's only one of many wild life reserves—anyone would think it was the Albert Hall or the Royal Command Performance!' he grinned.

Mrs Jefferson stiffened herself and looked shocked.

'The Jefferson Reserve is unique, Burt. There is none other so respected or quoted. It's a very responsible job Cary has given Rayanne, but my dear girl,' Mrs Jefferson turned to Rayanne again, 'don't worry. Cary wouldn't ask you unless he was sure you were capable of doing it. You see, we're always getting requests from quite famous people who want to come and stay here to see the Reserve and our experiments and also lecture. Cary always says *No* . . . he'll do the lecturing.'

'I doubt if he'd have asked me today if he hadn't to rush off to New York,' Rayanne said slowly. 'He must have been desperate to find someone at the last moment.'

'That's absurd, dear child,' Mrs Jefferson said slowly. 'Cary knew for several weeks that he was going to New York.'

Rayanne's legs suddenly felt weak so she sank into a chair.

'You mean . . . you mean Cary knew all along that he would be away?'

'Yes, dear, he did. He was annoyed because

183

he had to go before the end of the course, but they refused to postpone the meeting. It's extremely important—something to do with a big reserve in South America.'

'So he could have arranged for anyone to lecture,' Rayanne said slowly.

'Of course, dear. He could have phoned anyone and they could have flown up. No trouble at all. But he wanted you.'

'What do you mean, he wanted me?' Rayanne asked. She was suddenly afraid. Was it because it meant even more decisively that he didn't like her? That he wanted her to look a fool, to make her realise just how dumb and stupid she was? That would mean he was like all men—like her father and her five brothers!

'He told me ages ago that he thought you would make a good . . . what was his expression? A somewhat funny one, dear girl. I've got it: *channel.* He said you would make a good channel between the students and him, that they would find you more interesting and more sincere because of your age. You're very young, you know, Rayanne dear,' Mrs Jefferson added tenderly as she took her place at the table again and began eating.

'I suppose I am . . .' Rayanne said thoughtfully. Young to a man of thirty-five! 'I'm no good at talking, though. I'm always scared stiff I shall start saying *M'm . . . Ugh . . . Hum . . . er . . .'*

'Nonsense,' Burt sounded annoyed. 'You

talk very well. You must have been given plenty of notes by Cary. He's so methodical.'

Rayanne glanced at him. Was he being sarcastic? Why had he suddenly taken a dislike to Cary? she wondered.

'Yes, he has, but I'm only to use them as a tie-up of the other lectures. He wants me to tell them of my own experiences here, my own feelings.'

'Well, what's wrong with that? Make a good beginning for your much-discussed thesis,' said Burt, even more sarcastically.

Rayanne looked at him worriedly. It was so unlike Burt. Was he upset about something?

'I'm going over to young Warrender's house this morning,' Burt said curtly. 'Coming, or do you want to prepare for this afternoon?'

Hesitating, Rayanne thought fast. She wanted to go with Burt, because she hated him to be hurt in any way: on the other hand, she had a lot of thinking to do.

That afternoon! How it hovered above her head, coming closer every moment.

'I think she should study her notes, Burt,' Mrs Jefferson interrupted quietly. 'After all, there's always tomorrow.'

He stood up, a strange smile twisting his lips. 'Of course there is—but how many tomorrows will there be?' he asked, and left them.

Alone, Mrs Jefferson smiled at Rayanne. 'Don't look so worried, dear girl. Cary

185

wouldn't have asked you to give that lecture if he hadn't complete faith in you.'

Later, alone in her room, standing before the mirror and trying to start her talk, Rayanne wished she had faith in herself. If Mrs Jefferson was right, Cary not only trusted her but had had this in mind for some time. That meant he believed she could do it.

She stood in front of the minor and glared at herself.

'I'm here this afternoon to take the place of Cary Jefferson. I'm sure, like me, you're sorry about this, but he has been called away on an important visit to New York. He has given me some notes to tie up his previous lectures, but . . .'

She stopped and buried her face in her hands. How ghastly it sounded! Her voice all hoarse and croaky like a frog's. And pompous! That was the only word to describe it—smug and pompous. How on earth was she going to face all those critical faces of students waiting to see what she was like?

It was even worse that afternoon as Hubert Ellingham, in charge of the students, led the way on to the dais, introducing her to the students as they sat, notebooks open on their laps, looking up at her. Rayanne caught her breath with dismay, for in the back row she could see not only Burt, but Christine Horlock talking to him.

After being introduced, Rayanne stood up.

She looked at the faces before her.

'I'm sorry Cary Jefferson couldn't be here,' she began, and meant every word of it. 'He has asked me to tie up the lectures he has already given you, but first I'm to talk about my own experiences here. I hope you won't be bored.' She leaned on the tall lectern on the dais, her hair falling forward over her face, so she swept it back with an impatient gesture. She watched the ripple among the heads before her as they looked at one another and grinned. 'Please try not to fall asleep,' she added, and was rewarded with a chuckle that also seemed to ripple round the room. She took a deep breath.

'I came here,' she said, beginning to walk up and down the dais, using her hands as she spoke, demonstrating with her movements, 'as a sceptic. I'm afraid I had little interest in the conservation of wild life. I felt the money would be better spent on the feeding of the many millions of starving children and people in the world . . .'

Another ripple of approval from her audience filled the hall and some even clapped and one shouted: *Hear, hear.*

'But since I've been here . . .' Suddenly she knew she had to make them understand—that it was necessary, not only to Cary but to the whole world, to make them realise the good these reserves were doing, the knowledge that they were given by experiment in water and

187

soil conservation and that could be used . . .

She began to talk earnestly, seeing the faces before her as blurs, yet knowing she held their interest. She walked up and down the dais, moving her hands, pausing as she waited to let them accept something she told them.

It came as a surprise when Mr Ellingham touched her gently.

'Time's up,' he said.

'Don't stop!' someone shouted from the audience, and there was a sudden roar as everyone clapped. Rayanne stood, silent for a moment, looking at them.

'Thank you,' she said. 'Thank you very much indeed. I'm afraid I got carried away. I forgot about time.'

'Go on forgetting!' someone shouted.

But Mr Ellingham was standing up, pointing to his watch. Tea time!

'Can I quickly read what Mr Jefferson wanted tied up?' Rayanne asked.

Hubert Ellingham nodded and Rayanne quickly read aloud Cary's notes. How much better than my words, she thought, and then it was over, the students crowding out of the hall, some coming up to shake Rayanne's hand and to say she had given them a new slant on it.

Burt joined her and they walked back in silence to the house, Burt carrying the dispatch case that rarely left his side. Mrs Jefferson was waiting eagerly.

'I didn't come, dear, in case I made you

188

nervous,' she said. 'How did it go?'

'I got carried away,' Rayanne admitted, sitting down and taking the cup of tea passed to her. 'I must admit I enjoyed it, but I . . . well, I just don't know how it went.'

Burt was opening his case, taking out a tape recorder. 'I've got it all here,' he said. 'Like to hear it?'

'Of course, of course.' Mrs Jefferson clapped her hands excitedly. 'How clever of you to think of this, Burt.'

He looked up, his face almost surly. 'Cary asked me to.'

'Cary did?' Rayanne's hand flew to her mouth. So he hadn't really trusted her, then? she thought. He wanted to hear just what sort of fool she had made of herself. And why was Burt still in such a difficult mood? Hardly talking to her, almost grunting, and looking as if the end of the world was coming.

'He certainly did,' Burt said crossly. 'Now listen.'

He switched on. They listened to the introduction and then Rayanne's voice came.

'I'm sorry Cary Jefferson couldn't be here,' she began. Her voice was filled with emotion. Rayanne caught her breath with dismay. She had betrayed herself—anyone listening must have known she loved Cary. She looked quickly at Burt and saw him staring at her, eyebrows almost touching, mouth a thin line, eyes full of despair.

Then Rayanne forgot him as she listened to her own voice. Why, she thought with amazement, it was quite good. Clear, warm, full of emotion . . she wasn't nearly as bad as she had thought . . .

They listened in silence until the end. Then Mrs Jefferson clapped her hands.

'That was very good, Rayanne, very good indeed. You almost convinced me!' she laughed. 'Cary will be pleased, won't he, Burt?'

'No doubt about that,' Burt said gruffly, closing the tape recorder and putting it away; then he stood up, murmuring something about seeing them later, and left the room.

'What's the matter with Burt?' Rayanne asked. 'I've never known him behave like this.'

Mrs Jefferson had also stood up. 'I have some phone calls to make,' she said with a smile.

They walked together to the door. 'Doesn't Burt seem to be behaving strangely to you?' Rayanne asked anxiously. 'I'm quite worried about him.'

Mrs Jefferson gave her a strange look. 'Well, my dear, if you don't know what's upsetting poor Burt, it's time you grew up. Or perhaps you should look in the mirror. Ah!' she said, her voice becoming gay as she opened the door. 'We'll be entertaining tonight, Rayanne dear. Several reporters are staying on, so I invited them over.'

'Reporters?' Rayanne echoed. 'What are

190

they doing here?'

'Cary invited them. He doesn't usually, but this time they were needed . . .' Mrs Jefferson said, and hurried down the corridor towards her room, bouncing like a little pouter pigeon, her eyes shining happily.

Rayanne watched her go, puzzled at Mrs Jefferson's happiness. She had been almost triumphant. Why? Rayanne wondered. Why?

CHAPTER NINE

The party that evening was something of a nightmare to Rayanne. It was true the reporters were all friendly men, but they asked her question after question—where was she born, about her education, what had made her interested in wild life conservation, until her head seemed fuddled with the questions.

The group of men stood round where Rayanne sat while Christine and Daphne were at the other end of the room, alone with Burt and Mrs Jefferson. As they left, Christine said sourly:

'A lot of fuss about nothing! Anyone can give a lecture,' and Daphne had added, giving Rayanne a strange look:

'Just as well you're not in the medical profession or they'd create like mad about all the publicity. Aren't you rather overdoing it?'

'I had nothing to do with it!' Rayanne said indignantly.

'Is that so?' drawled Daphne. 'Now who'd 'a' thought it!'

As they left, Burt by her side told her softly to ignore them. 'Both jealous as can be. They want to know why Cary has given you so much publicity when he hates it himself.'

Rayanne turned to him, her hands imploring. 'Please, Burt, what does it all mean? It makes no sense to me. Cary lying about having to go to New York at the last moment . . .'

'That's easy to answer. He wanted you to talk spontaneously—not after weeks of worried thinking. He was right, too. You spoke naturally and I reckon you're very articulate.'

'Why, thank you, Burt.' Rayanne was grateful and also relieved because he seemed in a happier mood.

Now he chuckled. 'Man, how they hate you! Those two dames, I mean. You've done more in a short while than they have done in months. You're the boss's pet—that's the way they see it. Spoilt, cherished, and used.' He walked past her quickly, leaving her to stare after him, puzzled.

Mrs Jefferson kissed her goodnight. 'I think it was a very good evening, my dear, I do hope you enjoyed it.'

'It seemed to me . . . well . . .' Rayanne sought for the right words as she walked with

Mrs Jefferson to her bedroom. 'Well, didn't I get a lot of publicity for a very small thing?'

'Small thing?' Mrs Jefferson sounded indignant. 'Nothing to do with Jefferson Wild Life Reserve is small!'

Alone in her bedroom, Rayanne went over the day thoughtfully. Now what was Cary planning? Why had he done all that? Surely he could have given her more time to plan the talk? Was it kind of him? Or was Burt right when he said Cary was wise, that he wanted the talk to come spontaneously? It was hard not to feel thrilled, she thought, as she lay in bed. Her voice had been infinitely nicer than she had thought—and to have all those reporters interested in her!

She laughed. What a child she must be still to allow such a thing to excite and please her!

Next morning, when she and Burt went to call on the Crisps, Burt was almost silent, back into the difficult mood Rayanne had noticed. She wondered if she should ask him what was wrong, but decided to leave it to him to choose his time.

Samantha welcomed them with open arms. 'I've got coffee all ready. Burt, Mike is in the office,' she said, quickly getting rid of him and tucking her hand through Rayanne's arm to lead her into the sitting-room. 'Everything's going to be great. There's nothing definite about it yet, but they were most sympathetic and understanding. Mike realised how much it

193

meant to me and I think he's quite keen to see how we . . . well, what it's like to have a baby. I just can't wait . . . we can make that part of the garden a play part. Sand and a tiny pool. It mustn't be deep, of course, and I'll have a net over it except when I'm with her . . .'

'You want a daughter?'

'Yes, to start with . . . we're going to repaint the guest room and . . . oh,' Samantha suddenly hugged Rayanne, 'thanks for suggesting it.'

'Actually I think it was Burt's idea.'

'Burt's a darling. Why not marry him? He's obviously in love with you and he'll make a good husband.'

Rayanne smiled weakly. 'But I don't love him.'

You probably could, in time. Oh, that reminds me. We found the note.'

'So Cary told me. Where was it?'

'In the rubbish heap. My girl found it under the sofa. It must have been blown down.'

Rayanne looked at the windows. It would have to be a strange draught or wind that could have blown the note under the sofa.

'Where did you leave it?'

'On the mantelpiece. Here.' Samantha jumped up in her white trews and shirt, and touched the clock. She frowned, looked at the window and the sofa. 'Seems rather odd to me that it could have blown there.'

'Seems very odd to me, too,' Rayanne

agreed.

Samantha looked at her thoughtfully. 'Still, my girl might have made a mistake. Maybe she found it in the grate.'

'Maybe,' said Rayanne. It didn't really matter. The main thing was that Cary knew now that she had been right. 'I was certain you'd never rush off without telling Mike.'

'Of course not. He'd have been worried sick,' said Samantha. 'I'm surprised Cary even believed I would.' She smiled. 'Look, Rayanne, may I poke my nose in where it has no right to go? Watch out. You've waving the flag for Cary Jefferson, aren't you?'

Rayanne's bright red cheeks were answer enough. Samantha sighed. 'Not that I blame you, though. He's really the . . . well, how can words describe it? Just one of those things, isn't it. But you haven't a hope. You do know that? Cary just isn't the marrying kind. Or perhaps I'd say, *shouldn't* marry. All they think about is their work.'

But if I could help him, Rayanne was thinking, if we could make a team. She had to smile. What a crazy thought! As if Cary would ever accept a woman to work with him. What was it he had called them? A *nuisance, a headache,* and even a *pain in the neck.*

It was three days later that Rayanne went to the lab to get some information for her thesis. She had begun to write, much on the same lines that she had spoken to the students,

195

but there were a few facts to be checked. As she walked into the lab Christine looked up, her face bright with anger. She was reading a newspaper and came to meet Rayanne, thrusting the paper into her face.

'I wonder you have the nerve to come in here! What's the idea? You had no right to tell the Press such a lie. Cary will be furious . . .'

'I don't know what you're talking about.' Rayanne, wishing she had never come to the lab, looked round a little wildly at the modern equipment. Cary was certainly not mean about such things . . .'

'It's a lie. An absolute outrageous lie!' Christine fumed on.

'Look, let me read it,' said Rayanne. She leant against one of the tables and read the printed news:

'Cary Jefferson, one of the well-known leaders of wild life conservation, hopes that the young biologist, Miss Rayanne Briscoe, whose lecture at the Jefferson Reserve was welcomed and admired by everyone, may work for him in future as he finds it difficult to fit in the lectures required by the courses with his necessary travels round the world. This is most unusual in many ways, for until now Mr Jefferson has rather shied away from women biologists, for no admitted reason. Miss Briscoe must have made an impression on him; one that she proved by her first lecture which was so successful.'

'But it's not true!' Rayanne gasped, lowering the paper.

Christine looked triumphant. 'Exactly. I told you so. But why did you tell such a lie? Cary will be furious.'

'But I knew nothing about it. The Press must be making it up. Unless Cary did . . .'

Christine laughed, an ugly contemptuous sound. 'Oh, yes! Then if so, what did you do to Cary? Twist his arm, or burst into tears and beg for the job?'

Rayanne clenched her hand that was holding the paper. 'Neither, and you know it. I'll let you have the paper back, but I must show it to Mrs Jefferson.'

'She'll be delighted. This is what she's been fighting for all the time. A sweet biddable little English girl to marry her wonderful son!' Christine laughed bitterly. 'How long will you last before he's bored to tears with you? Why, you're nothing but a . . .'

Rayanne turned and walked out of the lab. She was shaking a little. Who could have told such a lie? How would Cary react? Would he believe that she had nothing to do with it?

Mrs Jefferson looked anxious when Rayanne joined her on the *stoep*. 'Now what's happened, Rayanne? You look so upset.'

'Read this,' Rayanne said curtly, then blushed.

'I'm sorry—would you please read this, Mrs Jefferson? I can't understand it.'

197

Mrs Jefferson's glasses were hanging round her neck on a thin silver chain. Finally she got them on and slowly read the newspaper. Rayanne stood while she waited, staring blindly out of the window.

'I didn't tell the Press . . . it's just a lie,' said Rayanne, and heard the rustle as Mrs Jefferson put down the paper.

'But it's quite true, dear girl,' Mrs Jefferson said gently.

Rayanne swung round, her face startled. 'I don't understand.'

'Actually I don't think it should be in the papers yet. Cary could have asked you when he returned. He wanted you to give the lecture first as he said you had no confidence in yourself and it had to be proved—to yourself—that you could do the job. Of course you'll take it, dear. I'm so happy about it and it will be a great help for Cary. He's always getting tangled up with appointments overseas and his lectures. Now he'll be able to relax.'

Walking slowly to an armchair, Rayanne lowered herself into it. 'You mean, he really is going to offer me the job?'

Mrs Jefferson nodded. 'Yes. Of course you'll take it and it will be lovely to have you about all the year round. I shan't have to travel so much, because I won't be lonely any more.'

Rayanne tucked her feet under her. 'I can't . . . I mean . . . Well, it just doesn't make sense.'

'Why not, dear girl? You're clever, Cary says. Articulate, according to Burt West. You're interested in the work. I think you've been happy here. Or do you find it too lonely?' Mrs Jefferson's voice was wistful.

'I've been very happy here, but . . . I don't know . . . 'Rayanne brushed back her hair. 'I just can't believe it!'

Mrs Jefferson laughed softly. 'Neither can I, my dear. You'll be like the daughter I've always wanted.'

Rayanne had been thinking fast. 'But Cary hadn't heard me lecture. How can he know I'd be all right?'

'He never doubted it for one moment. He said you had an ideal voice and showed emotion when you talked. He can't stand speakers who stand stiffly and talk like robots. Is that the right way to pronounce it, dear girl? I always get so muddled with these new words. Now, I must go and see Jacob. He will plant the flowers just where I don't want them . . .' She stood up with some difficulty, leaning on the chair's arms and smiled at Rayanne.

'I'm so happy, dear girl, so very happy,' she said softly, and left the room.

Alone, Rayanne couldn't sit still. She got up and began to pace up and down. She would have gone outside, but the heat was at its height and she needed to feel cool in order to think.

Was it all a hoax? A funny kind of joke? she

asked herself. Yet how could Mrs Jefferson know about it unless it was the truth? Would Cary tell his mother if he didn't mean it?

The door opened and Burt stood there.

'Well?' he asked, his voice strange. 'So you know.'

'I know?' Rayanne looked at the newspaper she was still clutching. 'Oh, yes, I see, you've read it.'

'Seeing that I gave the information, I didn't need to read it,' Burt told her. He walked slowly towards her.

'You told them?' Rayanne caught her breath. 'Then it's all a joke? A funny kind of joke,' she added bitterly. 'A lie. Christine accused me of lying about it.'

'It isn't a lie,' Burt said, his voice lifeless. 'Cary asked me to tell the Press.'

'But . . . but . . . ' Rayanne stared at him. 'I just don't understand.'

A thin smile moved Burt's lips. 'Apparently—according to Cary—you don't exactly hit it off. He said you were always either aggressive or on the defensive. You seemed to see him as an enemy and you were on guard. Some tripe about women's equality. Is that right?'

Rayanne could feel the colour burning in her cheeks. 'In a way, yes.'

'Well, Cary said that if he offered you the job, you'd jump down his throat, accuse him of patronage or cruelly teasing you, and probably

200

refuse the job without even considering it. He said he failed to get through to the real you, that you wouldn't let him. He even thinks you hate him simply because he's a man.'

'I . . . hate him?'

Burt nodded. 'Absurd, isn't it? Well, Cary wanted you to know he was going to offer you this job for a few days before he came back. So I told the Press you were going to be offered it. You'll notice that I didn't say you would take the job.' He paused. 'But of course you will.'

Rayanne put out her hand vaguely and was absurdly glad to feel the back of an armchair. She felt dazed, unable to think properly.

'I see no *of course* about it,' she managed to say at last.

Then Burt moved—fast, surprising her, taking her in his arms, kissing her, his mouth hard against hers.

She struggled for a moment and then lay still in his arms, passive but not returning the kiss. He let her go abruptly and just caught her from falling. He gave her a strange look.

'Don't say you're sorry. I know it's not your fault.' He gave a funny little laugh. 'I was a fool not to have seen it from the beginning. You'll take the job all right.' He turned and left her standing there, silently staring at the closed door.

Somehow she got to her room, took a straw hat because of the sun and went out into the garden. She walked right down to the water's

201

edge and found a stone on which to sit.

A huge crocodile lay there, sleeping peacefully, but then, almost as if he had sensed her presence, he began to move. Slowly but with a frightening strength of purpose as he made his way into the water. Rayanne shivered, but still stayed where she was. It was very hot, the perspiration sliding down her face, her thin yellow dress clinging damply to her back. She had to think—she had to think!

It was a dream come true. Working with Cary.

Seeing him every day—or nearly every day, for he was obviously away a lot. Living in this lovely quiet place, having work she enjoyed. Maybe she could even write a book about it. She had always dreamed of one day being a writer . . . There was so much to tempt her.

But . . . and it was a very big *but*, wasn't she asking for heartache if she stayed? Suppose Cary met a girl he could respect and love, and brought her back as his bride?

If she stayed, Rayanne told herself, every day would increase the danger of heartache. Even if he didn't marry, the mere fact that he didn't *see* her would hurt her. Each day, she knew, she would love him more; and each day would make the final ending more painful.

On the other hand, had she the strength and courage to break away? To return to England, to get some miserable unrewarding job, and let the family tease and laugh at her again?

What a difficult question it was! She wanted to stay; with all her heart she wanted to stay. But if she did stay, what would it do to her heart? Break it?

CHAPTER TEN

Somehow Rayanne wasn't surprised, when she joined Mrs Jefferson for tea, to learn that Burt had gone.

'He asked me to apologise for not saying goodbye to you, dear girl,' Mrs Jefferson said as she lifted the Queen Anne silver teapot and carefully poured out the tea. 'He says he thought it was better this way. I imagine you understand.'

'Yes, I understand,' Rayanne said, her voice sad. Poor dear Burt, suffering as much as she was. If only she could have loved him! He was such a dear, so kind . . .

As the days passed, what was most embarrassing was the fact that Mrs Jefferson took it for granted that Rayanne would accept the job. So did the others. Samantha was thrilled, but she also said she felt Rayanne had made a mistake.

'This is dangerous driving,' she said, her eyes narrowed worriedly. 'You do know that? If you don't watch out . . . I mean, let's face it, he's married to his work.'

'I know,' Rayanne answered. 'I'm still not sure I'll take the job.'

Samantha laughed. 'You will,' she prophesized.

Alone one night Rayanne tried to come to a decision. She got out a piece of paper and put FOR and AGAINST at the top of the page. Then she carefully thought out and typed neatly.

She read the result, and then burst into tears. The list read:

FOR
I love him
I love his mother
I love the country
I love the work

AGAINST
He can only break my heart as he doesn't even see me.
I hate his sarcasm and stuffiness.
Would he ever treat me as an equal?
The antagonism of Christine and Daphne.

There was no answer. No answer at all. She felt tempted to pack her clothes and get away, right away, six thousand miles away where perhaps she could get a job that so enthralled her that there'd be no time to think of Cary . . . Wasn't that the most sensible thing to do? Wouldn't that be less painful in the long run? Yet how could she run away and leave Mrs Jefferson alone? And the job? How could she turn down the job?

Three days later, a letter came from England. Surprised, because her family, including herself, were all very bad letter writers, she saw it was from her mother. The contents startled her even more.

'My dear Rayanne,

Your father and I are delighted at the news that you have at last found what you have been looking for all this time. You can imagine how thrilled dear Uncle Joe is. He also talks of coming out to see you and to meet his old love, Mrs Jefferson, whom he can remember very well. I enclose the newspaper cuttings as obviously this is your first step on a career that could make your name known all over the world, so you may want to keep them. You can't think how proud we are of you, Rayanne. I always knew that one day you would prove yourself. Your brothers all send their love and say ' Bully for you'. Not a very gracious remark, but you know it means a lot for them to say that.

With love from us all, Mother.'

Rayanne's eyes were smarting with unshed tears as she carefully folded up the letter
205

before she looked at the many newspaper cuttings. The news seemed to have been in every newspaper in England. There was even a photograph of her. One she recognized immediately as taken by Burt.

Was Burt still in this? Had he sent the news around, knowing her father's name was well-known, as were the names of her brothers? Yet the papers merely quoted what had been written in the South African newspapers, though all expressed amazement at a girl being offered the post! Apparently Cary Jefferson was well-known as a permanent woman-despiser, or perhaps woman-avoider!

'Good news, dear?' Mrs Jefferson asked.

Rayanne looked at her, seeing a blurred figure. 'Yes, wonderful. The nicest letter I've ever had in my life.' Suddenly she was dancing round the room, singing happily. 'Just think!' she said, stopping in front of Mrs Jefferson, leaning down, one hand on each arm of the chair 'Just think—they're proud of me! They're proud of me for the first time in my life.' Her voice rose excitedly. Then she remembered something and stood up. 'Oh, and Mother says Uncle Joe wishes to be remembered to you and he hopes to come out and visit us.'

'Your Uncle Joe?' Mrs Jefferson looked excited. Her hand went to her hair. 'I wonder when he's coming. I must go to the hairdresser. Oh, my dear girl, isn't life exciting these days?'

206

But was it? Rayanne wondered that night as she went to bed. This had merely added another problem to the one she couldn't solve. Her family was proud of her. What would they say if she turned down the job?

The next day after she had been to see Samantha, Kwido drove her back. It was rather early for lunch and there was no sign of anyone in the house. Rayanne hesitated in the lounge, looking round, wondering where Mrs Jefferson could be. The sound of a door opening made her swing round. It was Cary.

'Why, Cary!' she exclaimed, and moved instinctively towards him with a betraying eagerness. Now as she coloured, she added, 'We didn't expect you yet.'

'I'm aware of that.' He closed the door and leaned against it. 'I've just been listening to your lecture.' His voice had no warmth, no approval in it.

'What did you . . . er . . . did you . . . Is it all right?' Rayanne stammered.

He frowned, those great tufty eyebrows moving. 'Of course it's all right,' he said, almost crossly. 'Why shouldn't it be? I knew you'd make a good speaker. Very articulate. The kind of voice one can listen to indefinitely.'

She blushed with pleasure. 'I'm glad you liked it. Cary, about this job . . .'

'What job?' he asked, staring at her.

'Well, the job of . . . . of lecturing for you

when you're away,' Rayanne said, suddenly nervous. Had it all been a joke of Burt's? A strange unfunny joke, but the result of knowing she didn't love him?

'Oh, that.' He moved forward, coming nearer to her with surprising quickness. 'I'm afraid that's off.'

'It's . . . off?' Rayanne went white, she could almost feel the blood leaving her face. 'You mean, you don't want me?'

It was like a slap in the face. All this time she had been trying to make up her mind, trying to decide whether it was better to grab at what happiness she could, even if the price was high to pay. And it was all off. The job was not to be hers. She would have to go away . . .

Her nose seemed to prickle—a frightening sensation, since it was usually a warning she was about to cry and crying was the very last thing she must do.

'Yes, I've been thinking about it. I'm often away for several weeks.'

'And you couldn't trust me?' Anger was sweeping away her dismay. They were back in Square One. 'Just because I'm a woman!'

His hands gripped her arms. 'Look, for crying out loud, will you stop this Liberation nonsense? It has nothing to do with your sex at all.'

'Then why . . .' She felt breathless and trembling, angry yet excited, a strange combination of emotions.

208

'Because I intend to take you with me,' he said.

'Go with you?'

He smiled. She caught her breath. If only . . . 'Of course. It's usual for a wife to accompany her husband.'

'A *wife?*' Rayanne could hardly speak.

'You are going to marry me, aren't you? I thought it was all arranged.'

'Arranged? You mean by your mother?'

He smiled. 'If it makes her happy to think so, why not let her? I knew as soon as I saw you, that day at the Crisps'. You looked so tired and frightened, I wanted to gather you up in my arms and kiss you, but I knew you weren't in the right mood. You were the girl I'd spent my life looking for. And you?'

'Why, Cary, I knew . . . I knew it was you, then, too. Oh, Cary, it can't be true. It just can't!' she gasped, her voice bewildered. 'This must be a dream and I'll wake up . . .'

His arms were linked now behind her back as he pulled her closer.

'Not a dream, Ray. It's real. Right from the first moment, I loved you, but it seemed absurd. How could you love someone you didn't even know?'

'That's how I felt, too. It was absurd, but . . .'

'It was true. My mother said at once that you loved me, but I didn't believe it. You were so aggressive at times, I often thought you hated me. Then there was Burt West. You were always together.'

'Burt's a darling. I like him, but . . .'

He frowned, his tufty eyebrows drawing together. This time she could do what she had always longed to do, lift her hand and gently stroke the thick hard brows. Then she traced her finger down his nose and either side of his mouth.

'There's just one thing, Ray,' he said. 'You know what you're tackling? A lonely life.'

'Lonely?' She laughed and put both her arms round his neck. 'Oh, Cary, if you knew how happy I am! How could I ever be lonely married to you?'